C000143306

Match of the Day

A tale of mischief, mayhem and the pursuit of love

Ted Lamb

ISBN: 9798524269331

Any references to historical events, real people, or real places are used fictitiously. Names, characters, and places are such stuff as dreams are made on. D.E.F. Lamb 21 Arthur Bliss Gardens Cheltenham GL50 2LN

June 21, 2002: the date of a crucial semi-final World Cup England v Brazil match, with the whole country at fever-pitch. A rumbustious riot following England's defeat leads to many revelations for one young man and is a turning point in his desperate and often hilarious attempts to hit it off with the so-far elusive opposite sex.

Chapter 1 Game on!

Some dates you never forget. There are familiar anniversaries such as birthdays, of course, and then the set pieces everyone knows, like Christmas. Other events people usually always remember are more individual, personal and specific. For example, I can remember the day I left school – the date, things that happened, everything.

Why such reminiscences pop up when they do is another matter. Sometimes it's easy to recognise what has prompted the memories, such as sights, sounds, even smells, it's said. Me, I recall June 21, 2002 vividly each time a Football World Cup series comes round every four years.

If you can remember that far back, you must be about as old as I am now. With the recollections of that day, I also remember turning my back, for the last time, on a town I knew I no longer needed. Although maybe it no longer needed me? And with this memory there's a twinge of sadness for the innocent person I can barely recognise on that fateful midsummer date, the day that ... oh well, I'll get round to that.

It had its high and low points, the year 2002: When I finally turned my back on the town on the way to the bus station via the Park, my chosen escape route for nostalgia's sake, the lakeside lawn looked somehow bare in its green and featureless freshness. Gone was a large, burned patch, healed by the curatorial skills of the park gardeners. But round the bowls green you could still see quite clearly that some of the railings were missing, the site of poor Roy Selincourt's crucifixion. Yes, some quite extraordinary things had come to pass in what most would judge to be an unexciting corner of England.

Especially on a day I find impossible to forget. Like switching on a DVD, once the memory is sparked, I can replay it all quite vividly.

***

You know those mornings you wake up and everything's perfect? You feel well. Really, really well. All's right with the world. Mostly when this happens it takes only a few moments for some niggling thought to come along and spoil this. Worries pop into your head, about as welcome as a hangover. But, curiously, on this morning there is nothing at all to trouble me. Not yet anyway.

It takes a little while to fully open my eyes. It is early, but already quite light. I roll over to look at the bedside radio alarm: nearly 6 am. I remember I have set it to go off quite soon. I remember at the same time *why* I have set it, which probably explains some of my feeling of content and growing excitement. Not long from now, in countable minutes in fact, England is playing Brazil in a soccer World Cup quarter final match.

And what's more, I can very soon watch the game as it happens. There's a live morning TV relay from the pitch in Shizuoka, Japan.

The occasion is quite remarkable. Hard to believe, I know, but England, Land of Hope and Glory, is actually in the closing battles, with a chance of winning and perhaps going on to take the whole world tournament like we last did in 1966, so everyone keeps telling me. All we must do is get past Brazil. This very morning!

I switch off the alarm before it has a chance to chime (the tune is *My Boy Lollipop*, a present from Mum) and roll back to look at the ceiling, its pattern of familiar and comforting cracks in the plaster. My waking stomach gurgles, part hunger, part anticipation. Well, the nation's honour is at stake, man. I mean, nobody in England is going to miss this match, are they? Even if they don't know the off-side rules they pretty much have to watch. Another deep gurgle. I guess my stomach thinks it is not getting enough attention.

Because of the time difference with Japan, today's game will be starting before most people set off for work. Millions have taken the morning off or have planned to watch the match live on TV in their workplace. A special day, then.

Another surge of pleasure comes and stays. Life is good. There is still a little time for me to spend a few more long moments caught up in the state of bliss, and perhaps even dream…

Midnight? Poppy? They are waiting there, as always. I just have to close my eyes. Sometimes there are other women too. Real ones I have met, or someone I've seen on telly or a film. But I always come back to one of my imagined 'best' two, Midnight or Poppy, in the end.

I have no idea how they first got into my head. Midnight is tall, quite broad-shouldered, a swimmer's figure, and dark with long hair like tarred rope. She is full-lipped and dangerous, a strong woman, a strong character. She always takes the initiative, hustling me behind a fence, or dragging me down in cornfields, sometimes with unsuspecting people just yards away. Poppy in contrast is freckled, sweet and fair and gentle, softness itself.

7

And then, all at once, Gay Gordon pops up. I don't actually want Gordon around, but he sometimes appears and has to be driven away. He is a mix of all the gay blokes I have ever met, with a special speculative way of looking you up and down. I'm afraid of him, I admit, because I know what he wants, a nightmare scenario I have had ever since somebody told me when I was only nine that such things happened. Even now I can imagine I'm squirming to avoid the contact, him grinning at my discomfort. Midnight, help! Poppy, help! But today is not the day for any of them. After all, what if I fell asleep and missed the match? I pull myself together, avoiding the point of no return...

But for just a moment before I hit reality again the two most important questions of my life float into my consciousness, as they often do in waking moments: They are, No1, who is my dad? And No2, when am I going to experience first-hand physical love?

There's also sometimes a third question, and it's this: does the second of those unanswered questions cover up a fact that I might be hiding from myself. I could be gay. Does still being a virgin, and a mighty confused one at that (I am, after all, 21) point to this? Seems to me there's a chance it could.

Some might wonder if there really can be 21-year-old virgins in the twenty-first century. I'm afraid there can. I'm the living proof...

But before I get too involved with this familiar train of thought, I hear the one thing that can really bring me back down to earth: Mum's cough.

It drifts up through the house, dry, tinny. I know she is suppressing it. If she allows the full hacking monster to take over, I know it hurts her. Hurts her a lot.

I have been listening to the cough for two years, and I know all its variations. It first made itself known after I finally graduated with a media studies degree from the local poly, now almost a university, that nobody seems to think entitles me to a job. Still, I finally got the degree after what I called my 'gap year'. One year at first, then a bit more, finally finding myself studying on the fringes of pack of teenagers who seemed far more boisterous and rude than my lot had ever been. It was a real achievement, that degree, even if it hasn't led to much else.

A few of my contemporaries at school and then college had taken gap years too, like me, some reappearing with deep suntans and occasionally deeper philosophical convictions, some going to university or college like me, some going into jobs here there and everywhere and some reappearing not at all, fading memories in the minds of all those content to stay in our small town. Many of the girls still left here are now pushing babies around. Me? I mooch mostly, currently on the dole, but I've had a few odd jobs in shops and electronics factories where nobody was quite sure what the bits of wire and bright plastic we fiddled with eventually went into. I mean, it could be missiles, anything. Our hands were smothered in thin grey mineral oil day in and day out. It penetrated the tiniest scratches and creases and gave us all horrible dermatitis. Oh, and I once worked in a bar. Just once.

None of this is particularly on my mind now, however. I push one leg then another out of bed and sit up, blinking in the sunshine blazing over the silhouetted roofline of the red brick terrace opposite. I check again to see the alarm really is switched off. The good mood is still there. Like I said, it doesn't happen every day.

***

I go downstairs in my second-best jeans and a new T-shirt, in honour of the day: dark blue but without overt signs of patriotic tribalism. The sitting room is full of the curiously sweet smell of Mum's sickness. I cross to the window to let some light in, but it is dark in here even so. The morning sun does not penetrate down here to street level, but in the afternoon if it is sunny the fronts of the houses opposite light up too and the bricks glow golden-red. Then the room is lighter. I hear movement from her direction and turn round.

"Well, hello my little early bird," she says softly.

She is propped up on an elbow, wide awake, looking up from the settee where she nests in her pile of pillows and duvets.

"What gets you up at this God-awful hour?"

Mum has a smile people call infectious. One side of her mouth has an almost imperceptible lift and there's a faint dimpling underneath it, no more than a shadow really, and her green eyes … well, they sort of flash, and then fade slowly, and I've seen often, often, that nobody can ignore it. They soon find themselves smiling as well. You would too. Really you would.

It can also sometimes be a sort of mocking smile too, sort of mischievous. It's … well, whatever it is, she can deliver one of these happiness-unlockers under any circumstances, and you realise too that she knows what she's doing with it. Most of all, you want it to happen again. And it lives on, that smile, despite her illness, the same as it ever was.

"Hello," I say. "You're awake. Any better?"

"Not really."

She lifts a hand to her mouth, and I must listen to her cough again. She manages to keep it gentle, watching me with wide eyes set in a pixie-like face which has a serious look as I cross to the kitchen.

But serious is not one of her best acts, and her voice drifts in as I start to make her tea and toast. I'm making more than she will eat, I know, but I think it's better she has a bit of real food than the tinned formula food Doctor Cohen has recommended 'to keep mum's strength up'.

"So, are you going to keep your dying mother company or are you off to the Tap?"

Her voice carries to me through into our long, narrow kitchen, which I sometimes imagine as a ship's galley. The Tap? Although many pubs, including the town's notorious King's Tap just mentioned, are indeed open early for business on this famous morning of Friday, June 21, 2002, I have already made up my mind I will stay and watch the game at home with Mum, a decision I might already be starting to regret. But I will go through with it: apart from anything else there is the embarrassing fact that I do not actually have the money this morning, at this time at any rate, to buy myself a drink. It is pay day for my unemployment cheque, but I will have to wait for the post to deliver that. By the time it comes and I can cash it in, the match will be long over. I'm also due to go in for one of my Jobcentre progress interviews this morning, by the way. Not on my favourites list. Anyway (as I told myself on the previous night when I made the stay-at-home decision), it is ridiculous to

11

drink at such an early hour simply because the big game is being relayed at that time from Japan, where it is now afternoon. Now isn't it?

"You're not dying Mum. I'll put the telly on in a minute. Do you want me to help you upstairs?"

It has been a long time since she has been able to go to the bathroom unaided. The stairs make her completely breathless.

"You are a good son, Petrovich," she says as I come back into the room. My name is Peter – Petrovich is one of her silly names for me. 'Peterkins', 'Petey' or even just 'Pet' are others.

"Perhaps you could just bring me a bowl of water and my things and help me wash. I can make do with the downstairs loo."

She watches me bring our breakfast on a tray, gravely serious again. It's a bit like being scanned by a store security camera. I put her cup and toast on the coffee table beside her and sit myself at the dining table, which we never used to eat at before she got ill.

"Can't you wash when Tania gets here?" I grumble.

Tania Watson is her home nurse. I genuinely don't like helping Mum wash, something deep I can't conquer.

"I suppose so." She sounds grudging. "You'll have to help me to the loo now though."

So, our toast must wait and it will be cold. Never mind, worse things happen at sea, which was one of my late Gran's favourite sayings in the face of various disasters.

Mum sits up carefully, arranging her nightdress, smoothing down the folds. She has become quite skinny with her illness, and it shows most on those gentle long fingers which have become thin and bony, bird-like.

She holds my arm – still a good grip – I help her up, and then we progress somewhat slowly to the toilet. I look at my my watch as we make our way there and I can see it is getting perilously close to kick-off time in Shizuoka.

With me propping her up from behind, the narrow hall gives her support on one side, and once we get to the loo, she can manage alone inside using the walls to manoeuvre. I wait for her, leaning against the hall wall and listening to her tinkle, followed by the rattle of the paper roll holder and then the flush, with a flurry of little coughs for the exertion of it all. Then we hobble back. I could have carried her she is so light. But her hair, which they told her she would lose for sure, is still thick and has steely-grey vigour despite the medication, a life of its own. If it was not tied back in a severe bunch, it would spring out wild, like wire. It told of stronger and healthier times – times not that far distant, really. Times when she sang. She hasn't sung at all recently. I remember folk songs, old pop stuff, sixties stuff really. Some of them I know because they replay them on the radio and new singers put them out on TV behaving as if they wrote them themselves. I think they should always write their own stuff.

Mum's illness? There is 'something on her lungs' – unfair really, because she never smoked, except for cannabis in her youth (she told me) when everybody did, so they say.

The doctors apparently fear the 'C' word more than her, for she knows it is cancer despite a fancier label. We both do. It means medication and now-and-then trips in an ambulance to the hospice where they do some rather more drastic chemical and radiation cell-blasting.

I'm sure if you picked her up and shook her she would rattle with all those pills inside her. She has a tablet-dispenser like a miniature toolbox, with all the doses measured out in compartments to be taken morning, noon and night.

Though no-one has said as much, every now and then the reality strikes me her recovery is a rather remote wish. For sure she isn't getting any better. The realisation makes me sad. Even now, my eyes begin to water as I settle her back on her settee. Mostly I try not to think about it. I remember Gran's slow decline from the same illness. Gran smoked about 60 a day, Capstan full strength untipped. She had it coming, we knew. You could hear her coughing a mile away even before she was ill.

With everything attended to, I switch on the telly and as an afterthought put a video tape cassette in the recorder. We were not up to speed on DVDs in those days.

The England manager, Sven Goran Eriksson, appears, bobbing here and there, all grins and glinting specs. I can't make him out, personality-wise. He is so foreign. It's widely known he has affairs, women flock to him. So what's his secret? Money? I certainly can't detect any of the attributes I think of as being sexy. Nothing I haven't got, I imagine. The same can't be said for the players, who are obviously handsome, young and fit, and they apparently have a whale of a social life as a result. They are all on screen now, warming up, jogging, doing back rolls and kicking their legs in the air, stretching. Nerves are being steeled; the tension is rising.

14

"Who are we playing?" Mum asks.

More mischief, you see, because she isn't that daft – she has been following the build-up all week. I don't answer.

"Petrovich, I asked you a question."

"You know, don't you?"

After that exchange we watch the pre-match build up in silence for a while.

Things will be in full swing in the Tap by now, I imagine – at least until the game starts. The thought of drinking cold beer at this hour, instead of the lukewarm tea and cold toast I am now consuming, makes my stomach lurch. I seem to remember bacon butties have been promised by the landlord too. Another tummy lurch. But perhaps after one or two beers the early boozing experience can't be all that bad. Alcohol is like that.

So we sit and watch, Mum and I, nibbling our cold toast as the teams jog about a bit more.

At last, kick-off is called.

I know the details of this game will be pored over for days and weeks to come, so I watch carefully. The opening play has a sort of entertaining flow to it. Mum 'ouches' and 'oohs' at the missed shots and near things, cheers and laughs with England's goal, and breathes in sharply when goalie Seaman crashes down on his neck from a high leap. But from that point on, just before half time, we seem to be giving it all away. That doesn't matter so much to Mum. She is obviously cheering for both sides.

We lose the match 2-1, as you probably know. It ends in tears, mostly from captain Beckham.

Do not run away with the impression from all this that I am a soccer aficionado – I am not, and I never have been. It's just that this particular World Cup series, England has come so far that overall victory actually seemed to be attainable once this quarter-final was out of the way. The national build up has been terrific. Everybody has been talking about it, even people who never dreamed of watching a football match before.

When it is all over, I feel a curious sense of elation despite the defeat. I have watched the game, I have taken part in the national shared experience of it all, and that gives me the passport to be able to talk about it with everyone I run into today. Valuable currency. I have a recording of it too, I remember, and I switch the video machine off and take out the tape, although I leave the TV on for a bit for Mum to watch.

While it does not matter to me deeply that we lost, I do know what others might feel, people who really follow the game. A cruel blow for lots of people in fact. Never have so many been let down by so few, so suddenly. Maybe I do have just a twinge of disappointment.

It is different for Mum. The downcast faces and tears of the players and fans and the subdued voices of the commentators are objects of her scorn, not sympathy.

"Look at them," she announces. "It's only a bloody game. How silly!"

To be fair, shut inside as she is and sheltered from everyday existence, she couldn't truly know the real depth of feeling about this match in the country at large. I mean, I asked her about 1966, the last time England won the World Cup, and she said she didn't really remember anything about that one except people had kept telling her to buy commemorative red, white and blue postage stamps with 'England winners' printed all over them. They could become valuable, many believed. She hadn't bought any though. Just as well. Others had stormed the post offices, and nobody had been any better off from doing so, because thousands and thousands of stamps were set aside by people greedy to have something for nothing. They no longer had any real scarcity value.

"What about the England players?" I ask her, trying to awaken some empathy in her. "They must be really upset, Seaman, Beckham and all the others..."

"Beckham? Is he the one with the spiky hair? He's really sweet, isn't he?"

"What about Cole?" I try.

"The black one? Mmm, he's nice. Big. Firm. Lovely bum."

"Mum!" I feel a flush of embarrassment. She isn't seeing things in quite the way I do.

"I do like those Brazilians too," she goes on. "Very tasty."

A laugh sets off another series of dry coughs, and she grabs at the back of the settee and holds on, as if the spasms are about to dump her on the ground. Or perhaps it is just the pain makes her hold tight, I can't really tell.

"Oh dear, Petrovich," she says when she gets things back under control. "It's a bit fierce today."

"The pain?"

"No, no, not the pain. No, that's all right. It's the rest of it. Feels sort of different today. Maybe."

There's a gap in our conversation. The experts on the telly have now started pulling the whole game to pieces blow by blow. When they have done that, they do it all over again. I can see they will probably go on and on like this for the rest of the day. I switch off, clear things away. She has managed to eat a piece of toast, at least. Then we get out her morning collection of pills on the coffee table and she sends them down one by one with gulps of cold tea.

"Is there anything special you want when I'm out?" I ask, bringing up the subject of my intended departure.

I hope that the thought of having a treat brought home will take her mind off the grimness of swallowing so many chemicals.

"Lamb chops perhaps?"

Lamb chops are her favourites, more so since her illness. For most of my life she – we – had been vegetarians. This had stopped suddenly one day in the year I was 18, when she brought home four lamb chops, cooked them and served them as if they were nothing out of the ordinary.

"Aren't they beauties," she said (I can remember the words exactly). She was strangely bright-eyed. She had folded her fork and knife together afterwards and taken no notice of my curiosity at this sudden change in diet.

"Lovely. From Roger Stenton. The butcher on the corner – you know."

Thereafter chops appeared from time to time, never anything else in the meat line and always from Stenton's, the corner shop where our street, Morris Street, joins Victoria Road, the main road into town.

I can see she is thinking over my offer to bring something back for her as if it is some sort of battle of will she has to overcome. She gives in with a little smile, almost like surrender. "All right then."

Her voice has deepened, and I don't know why but it somehow makes me feel embarrassed again. I turn away.

"You'll get them from Stentons, Peter?"

Her voice is almost back to normal. "I will," I say. "Anything else? Cakes? Some ice-cream? I'll get my cheque today if you want to borrow."

"No, no," she says. "We don't need to buy anything more yet (I do a supermarket shop once a week from a list she writes). But be an angel and get mummy one of her little drinkies, will you?"

She reaches out and pats my leg as I pass.

Her eyes are large now, and mockingly grave. "Be careful Peterkins, my pretty little boy," she says. "The world out there is full of wicked women."

How I wish it was! I get the gas ring going, start to make up one of her formula drinks with hot milk.

The doorbell rings just as I am finishing this. I hear it opening almost immediately – Tania has her own key. When I bring back the drink Tania has taken my chair so that she can drag it over and sit beside Mum.

"Hello Peter. How has Mrs Walker been?"

Tania is one of those people who speaks as if mum isn't in the room. I feel like saying "Why don't you ask her?" Instead I swallow and say: "Fine Mrs Watson. Aren't you Mum?"

Mum can never be relied upon to be so kind as me, although the manner adopted by the ample-figured West Indian nurse is not entirely her own fault I guess – in the many situations she meets on her support nursing rounds there must be be worse cases than Mum, cases where relatives and carers are the only people who can answer for their far-gone wards.

"I suppose I am if Peter says so, Tania."

Tania either choses to be thick skinned or does not notice the tartness, which is laid on plainly enough for me to pick up.

"Are we taking all our rations?" Tania quizzes, again with a look at me rather than Mum.

I flinch, watching Mum take a breath for what could be another rather short delivery. When it comes it is rude enough but not too bad.

"Want some too, do you?"

Tania has to look at Mum now and makes a face. "No, I don't think so. They'll do you more good than me."

Greetings over, Tania becomes brisk and business-like.

"Now, what can we do for Mum while we're here?"

It's the chance I have been waiting for. "Perhaps you can help her wash? I must go out. Appointment, I'm afraid. By the way, did you watch the game?"

"Game – what game?" says Tania.

Clearly not then.

"No matter."

I leave them sparring gently and go to my room to get the stuff I need for my Jobcentre interview.

Chapter 2 Escape

My bedroom is the biggest of the two upstairs rooms in our house: Mum gave it up to me when she gave up having a double bed, on account of the fact I needed a desk for college work. On the desk is a second-hand PC and a printer badly in need of a new ink cartridge, but the rest of the desktop is clear, the way I like it.

There are three drawers, the shallow one over my knees full of biros, pens, rulers, the maths instrument set I kept from school, various odds and ends. The deeper top drawer to the right has writing paper, envelopes and stuff, and the one underneath that has watercolour paints (tubes and tablet sets) and sketch books.

I don't think I'm a bad artist. I mean, I have seen a lot worse, especially when the town art society puts on a display in the park every year. There are a few complete pictures in some of my books, like vase of sunflowers and an older picture of the tabby cat we once had before it got obliterated by a joyrider on the road just outside. Those are the are particularly good ones. Most of all though I enjoy doing landscapes, usually imaginary ones because I never seem to have time to go out and sketch. The last one I started, I'm sorry to say, had to abandon after I showed it to Mike Collins, a former friend. I'd been rather proud of it to that point.

"Ha!" he exclaimed on picking it up out of a corner one day and holding it at arm's length. His exclamation was not without mirth, which wasn't at all the reaction I was hoping for. I wanted something more like the acclaim Constable would have attracted when he first showed someone *The Haywain*. To me the watercolour has a sort of satisfying completeness: two rounded hills, with a brook running from the central valley folds and emerging under a foreground bridge, with a little cluster of bankside bushes.

"Hey," continued Mike, who is always inclined to let things run away with him when he gets going. "You know what this looks like? Tits, these hills. And a fanny, here."

He jabbed a finger at the bridge.

"Half shut your eyes. See Pete? You don't do totem poles too, do you? Hey, how about having a log, a bloody great log, floating out under the bridge? Penetration, as it were. That would really do it."

I could have hit him. Did being an art student give him the right to poke fun at my untutored but, I feel, competent efforts? I was totally embarrassed. A really cringing hot flush came over me and I hurriedly took the picture off him, changed the subject. When he had gone, I searched all my other pictures to see if they too carried similar undercover interpretations. I don't think they do, unless you look very hard and have *that* sort of imagination.

All the same Mike wounded me. I never felt the same friendliness towards him after that even though he had been a mate since primary school. He was very greasy and pimply, I noticed in the new light in which I regarded him and had bad breath and dirty fingernails to boot. Always.

I have never looked at that picture again. In fact, I haven't picked up a paintbrush since. It's a fag, anyway, getting everything out then having to clear up afterwards. For the moment I am resting my artistic talents, just like my writing. If I boot up the computer a screen splattered with folders points to writing I have started and postponed, with just a few pieces complete and waiting revision. Painting or writing could well be my future, but both are for the moment on hold. Sometimes in the Tap or some other place with lots of people and babble all around I feel like Prince Harry in *Henry the Fourth, Part One*, which we had to do in school. You know, "I know you all and will a while uphold..." and he's content to put off being a leader and just arse around for the time being but promising himself it won't be forever. In the meantime, it's all experience, isn't it? I mean, there is plenty of time to get back to all that.

My other belongings are a music system and stack of CDs and, in the corner and, unused for a considerable time, some fishing tackle. I have been promising myself to go fishing sometime because I once got huge if solitary enjoyment from sitting on river banks. But the moment has not yet come round.

There's a guitar too and although I can play some simple chords slowly, I sort of know I'm going nowhere with music. Song writing, perhaps, but not music. Mum on the other hand can string chords together well, and sing too, as I said. I mean, she used to.

A cardboard concertina file beside the desk holds all my important papers and letters. In it I find the items I needed for my interview, which I put in a used brown envelope frugally saved for just such a use. I check in Mum's old dressing table mirror that my number two haircut isn't getting unfashionably long and decide I can skip a shave. I pull the duvet into a tidy shape, pocket my pay-as-you-go phone (large and brick-like, and not topped up for several months now so practically useless) and leave the room.

23

When I slip past the sitting room doorway the conversation between Mum and the nurse has become a low murmur. Harder I guess to spar successfully when you're one-to-one and in a vulnerable position. I pick my cotton jacket off a hook in the hall. A handful of letters lies on the doormat as I had hoped. I grab the familiar-looking buff one I know to be my Benefits handout cheque, leave the rest of the letters where they are and step out of the front door into a glorious morning.

Often, like now, it is a huge relief to leave, shut the door on all that, leave it behind me.

Today though I am feeling more than that. It's going to be a really special day, I can tell. Big events in our town come and go, and mostly they fizzle out from lack of interest: Royal weddings and funerals, the turn of the millennium, that sort of thing. Not today.

I am looking forward to meeting just about anyone because of the big football game. Everyone will be talking about it.

Chapter 3 Warm-up

I start walking into town and stop when I get to Singh's corner shop to buy a *Guardian*. Somebody once told me the *Guardian* is balanced and anti-establishment. I don't really understand how it can be both.

In the shop there's a heady atmosphere of curry spice mixed with printer's ink and overlaid with overripe fruit. Mr Singh, behind the counter, asks me how Mum is, then launches enthusiastically into a sales pitch, urging me to buy a *World Cup Special* edition printed by the *Argus*, our local paper. He is very insistent. I think the paper's circulation people must have been on at him to push it hard.

The *Argus* has just rushed out this edition on the game Mum and I have been watching. Isn't it wonderful, Mr Singh says, how quickly they can do these things now? "Truly amazing when you think of it!" Really, does anyone ever think about such trivia? Does anyone care? But he holds it under my nose, and it is sort of impossible to refuse.

I take out money to pay him and I'm on the brink of opening a conversation about the match when, through the open door of the dully lit depths of the storeroom behind him, one of his daughters appears.

This plunges me into panic: it is the roly-poly one. There are several Singh daughters, of all ages, shapes and sizes, but all are dark-eyed and all exceedingly attractive. I don't know her name or the names of any of her sisters. Somehow, despite there being so many of them, not one was ever in my classes at school or college.

Why the roly-poly one always makes mischief with me I can't say. Perhaps she does it with everyone. She is the worst of the lot. This time I can see I am in for trouble again. She looks at me over her father's shoulder, grins broadly – not a smile, a grin – cups a hand under each of her plump breasts and jiggles them at me under her loose T-shirt. Mr Singh has no inkling any of this is going on and appears to be saying "Hello" to me all over again, even though we have already exchanged greetings and our transaction is all over except for me taking the small change he is now offering.

"Hello," I say again, flushing, looking at his face and trying to get the provocative background feature to drop out of focus. The only way of doing this effectively is to look at my nose and make myself cross-eyed.

"Hello?" he says again, pushing the coins towards me. I repeat the greeting back again, adding "Hi" for good measure. An odd sad air of exasperation comes over his face. He speaks again, this time slowly and deliberately, the way people talk to small children or idiots.

"Do-you-want-to-take-your-mother's-*Hello*-too?"

Oh god! Now I'm embarrassed by my lack of comprehension.

"N...no," I say, realising finally he is talking about Mum's *Hello* magazine.

Mr Singh looks relieved he has finally got his message over. Why do women have this unhealthy taste for showbiz gossip? I mean, what's the attraction? I can appreciate the pictures of pretty women ... I'm a man, after all. But surely women don't feel the same way. Do they? And as for what they get up to, why, it isn't any more than you see on Eastenders, is it?

"Thanks all the same Mr Singh. But not now. I'm on my way to town."

I take the change, try to regain some composure and uncross my eyes.

But to my horror not one but two brown girls now swim into view. A skinny younger one has joined her sister. They are both enjoying the proceedings mightily, all four tits now dancing in a sort of chorus line, the evil little blighters sniggering together. Both girls wave as I turn to go, grinning even more. In my confused hurry, I stumble on the doorstep. I hear the paper rip as I steady myself with a hand on the doorpost. But I dare not look back.

When I am out of range of my tormentors, I realise I did not say anything to Mr Singh about the game. I had gone into the shop I resolving I would make my first match comment to him, perhaps opening a conversation. No matter. There is still plenty of day left and without doubt plenty of people to see.

I head for the park and by degrees the Cheshire-cat image of whatever-her-name-is's grin fades and I start to feel a little better, a bit more like I felt when I left home.

The traffic is quite heavy.

There is a sort of mini-rush hour in progress with people going to work after taking time off to watch the game at home, I suppose. I pass one or two pubs. They all seem to be full and noisy, with loud televisions still blaring away. The pundits and analysts, both in the bar and on TV, are undoubtedly playing the whole match over yet again, analysing every kick and stumble.

***

Victoria Park is a nice place to slip into at any time of the day, except perhaps in the gathering dusk, for several very good reasons. The legacy of a bakery magnate long gone to either the balmy proving rooms above or the roaring ovens below, it lies between our residential area, Southfields, and the central business and shopping area. This is clustered around another period piece, the Victorian red brick Town Hall and covered market complex, the former being part of an ornate palace including function rooms known as the Vic, or more properly the Victoria Rooms, where the Beatles had once played. Fading framed photographs in the foyer verify this single claim to fame.

I look for a bench in the sun by the boating lake close enough to smell the water and see darting dragonflies, the next best thing to sitting on the bank and fishing, and I look properly for the first time at my *Argus* special.

The front page has one big picture of England team captain David Beckham sitting on the grass with his head between his knees. A very good picture, I think, the embodiment of grief. A big headline states: "THE DREAM'S OVER".

The fact I have managed to rip the desolate captain nearly halfway through in my escape from the demon Singh girls makes it even more poignant.

But before I have a chance to open the paper I am interrupted by a drawled local greeting, a woman's voice, high and nasal, with a detectable local burr. If you lived here for any length of time, you'd know a town accent anywhere.

"Hiya Pete."

Carol Latham, pushing a baby buggy. I don't remember ever seeing her smile at me quite like that before. Wide, and sort of glad to see me – that is the description that comes to mind. Happy too. There is something of that in there. I'm puzzled by this.

"Lovely day," she says.

She slows down but doesn't stop. The child is asleep.

"Yes," I agree. "Great."

What am I saying? England has just been put out of the World Cup!

Carol and her baby continue on their way, and I look out over the lake. There are black and white house martins skimming the surface. When I look round again Carol is looking back at me over her shoulder. She turns her head forward quickly and carries on. I look back to the gyrating birds.

The martins and swallows came in late in this year. The weather has been cold and wet, keeping them in France until this sudden spell of sun. A fish flips in the brown stillness of the lake's surface, scattering a spray of sunlit droplets into the air. One of those moments when time seems to slow down.

It hasn't been a boating lake for years, though it is still called that. There was even a swimming area once, until someone caught polio there.

I turn back to the *Argus* football special. As specials go it is a bit of a cheat, just the front and back and a couple of inside pages on the game, wrapped round the ordinary paper. But there is a fairly accurate report on the match. It seems very well written for local journalism. I guess the story could have come with the picture over the wire, or over the internet, whatever papers use these days.

"Hiya."

Not many minutes have passed but it is Carol again, now passing in the opposite direction, with her child, Toby I think he is called, just awake and stretching. It is a matter of much local speculation as to who the father might be. One thing I can say for certain is it wasn't me.

Being reminded virginity can bring on attacks of heartburn which have been getting worse lately. It is sometimes embarrassing. I must try hard to think of something else, anything.

Carol was in the same form as me at the town comprehensive. She has always been attractive in a sort of pouty way. Like all the other girls who weren't what Mum called 'somewhat plain' she had gone out for a spell with Richard Jones, a dark high-cheekboned Welsh boy – it was rumoured there was no question he had lost his virginity before leaving primary school (a bubble of acid stirs – even bringing the V-word to mind can do it). Richard married at 17. He's now separated and a bit of a drunk. The girls still fancy him though. All this happened long after he split with Carol, so he isn't the father of her child, most people tell you.

The other thing that makes Carol popular is that she is a blonde – at least since primary school she has been. Today she has her hair piled up and pinned but the carefully designed stray curly wisps, like springs, which tumble from her temples, speak of much preparation.

As she walks away it occurs to me that she has become broader, and my eyes are drawn in her retreat to the butterfly tattooed just above the waistband of her jeans. She is in one of those little sleeveless knitted tops, pink, which exposes several inches of bare midriff all round.

At this moment Toby starts yelling. He isn't the only one in Vic Park who doesn't know who his father is, is he? Only in my mum's case, I'm pretty sure she knows. Will I ever get it out of her now? Sometimes it seems the most important thing in the world to find out, sometimes not.

I look up from this reflection to see Carol has turned yet again and is heading back with some determination. It is my turn to look away.

This time, however, she really homes in on me and sits down confidently beside me. She starts lifting the wailing child out of his straps.

"Hungry," she says, looking swiftly round the park. There is hardly anyone else here at all, just a strolling middle-aged couple some distance away. Suddenly things feel unreal, close and intimate. Then to my horror she starts to roll up the jersey thing one-handed and once again that day I find myself staring at breasts, this time bare, full and pink-nippled. Moist too.

"Did you watch the game?" she asks, matter of fact, while she draws Toby's wet and working lips towards his goal. I can't look anywhere else. A warm milky smell, not unpleasant, wafts at me.

A new wave of embarrassment sweeps me – I know I am blushing; I know I am staring at her tits, and I know I will stammer.

"Y-yes. Did you see it? It was awful, wasn't it?"

31

Making myself cross-eyed again, I try to look at Carol's face alone.

"Yeah. I was in the Tap," she said. "Terrible. Didn't that goalie hurt himself ever? And poor Becks – he cried after, didn't he ever? Mum was babysitting for me. That's why he's a hungry boy, isn't he. Missed your breakfast, didn't you?"

In one breath her voice goes from adult to baby-burble. She looks down at the suckling Toby, doting, instantly forgetting the game. "There's alcohol in that, baby," she says. "Make you sleep … 'opefully."

The middle-aged pair I first saw much further away are passing us now, smiling, and Carol looks up, smiles back. I realise they probably think we were together, an item, a happy little family scene. Perhaps Carol thinks this too? She seems pleased with the effect, but the mixture of pride and horror that comes over me is confusing and brings on a fuller, deeper flush than I think I have ever felt before. Even the embarrassment I felt over my painting.

"I .... I have to go," I stammer.

I snatch up the newspaper and my envelope, rising and starting to walk.

"Appointment. Jobcentre. Must go," I gabble over my shoulder.

Uncrossing my eyes, I see she has that smile again. I also notice for the first time her face is soft and downy in outline, like a peach skin.

"Seeya soon," she says – the local sign-off.

When I look back from the park gate she waves, still holding Toby up to her breast with one hand. The strolling couple are watching me go too. No doubt they are also smiling, but it is too far away to see.

Well, my first game conversation, albeit a somewhat brief and unexpected one. Hopefully my next port of call will present a better chance of getting into something rather deeper - although it occurs to me also that I have perhaps been a bit dismissive of Carol's grasp of football tactics by not opening up the topic further. Am I unfair to women perhaps? Is this my problem? Mum's always accusing me of being a chauvinist, but I don't think I am. I mean, I try consciously not to be. What more can you do?

***

Our Jobcentre, like all Jobcentres, I realise, is as familiar as school used to be. It is in the same type of prefabricated building, and it even has the same institutional smell. One component of this aroma could be fear. You don't always feel comfortable coming in, though for some time, for me at least, things here have not been all that bad. But there are plenty of people who tell of awful experiences.

It is never worth looking at any of the cards they put up on boards. I don't know anyone who got work off them and all the reasonable jobs are in the *Argus* anyway, so anyone in my position, i.e., long-term unemployed, wastes no time on them and goes straight to the rank of bolted-down grey plastic chairs by the interview area.

Roy Selincourt, I see, is already seated there, a leg in plaster (he has always broken one limb or another, or if not a limb a rib, or a finger or something else). In the corner sits an overweight and dishevelled balding man with grease spotted clothes and a broken metal specs frame. He is often there, and never appears to be called up for an interview. He never answers anyone's greetings either, so by degrees people have stopped bothering to say anything to him. Perhaps he just likes being there, like a piece of the furniture. And it's warm and dry.

I don't know how Roy had got into the college at about the same time I did, but it was said at the time they would take anyone because government funding depended on the numbers of students on their books. Nowadays, sometimes he is still studying, sometimes he is unemployed, like now I guess. It isn't unusual for me to find him here at the Jobcentre. Our interview times often coincide.

"Hi Roy," I say, adding the appropriate Jobcentre inquiry, "Been waiting long?"

Sticklike Roy has never graduated in anything. I don't even remember what he currently studies. He is rarely at college, just as he had rarely been at school and as a consequence gathered no GCSEs or A-levels. Most of the time, in any circumstances you can name, Roy is off sick.

That said, he is likeable. In fact you couldn't find anyone with a bad word for him. But he always makes you worried because he is so fragile.

"No," he replies. "Just got here. I was in the Tap. See the game?"

Ah! A chance for my first serious game conversation.

But it is not to be. Not yet anyway, for my name is called almost immediately.

Alan Jones, sometimes called 'Joker' Jones, and a year younger than his drunken Lothario brother Richard, is not a nice man, the nickname belying his constant sourness. I couldn't say whether this has anything to do with his brother's contrasting social successes or simply a sour genetic disposition. Whatever, he is not the sort of bloke you want interviewing you at the Jobcentre, and when he appears at one of the screened windows and looks at me my heart sinks.

"Walker!"

He doesn't have to call out like that. A nod will do, or at least my first name. He knows who I am well enough too, what with being another contemporary at school – him the quiet kid who never joined in. Oh well, I think, better make the best of it. Of all the Jobcentre staff I would have preferred the much nicer and certainly prettier Miss Strensham, but no matter. I go up and sit facing the grille.

"Let's see, Peter John Walker, isn't it?"

I think, *'for fuck's sake, Joker, you know, don't you? You heard it called off the school register enough times'*. He opens my fat dossier on the counter in front of him and starts going through it, holding his head in his hands when he is not turning pages so that all I see is the prematurely balding top. I wonder if he has ever forgotten the surprise vicious dead-legs I used to give him in the school playground. Everyone did that to him. Perhaps we all turned him into a bitter, twisted nerd.

I decide to lift the proceedings and go for an informal approach.

"Hi. Nice morning. Did you watch the game?"

"Good morning," he says frostily, looking at me as if I am some kind of garden pest. He's got more to say...

"I assume you mean the World Cup match this morning. No, this is a busy government office, Walker, not the private sector where people take time off for the silliest things. And we don't have all the free time in the world like unemployed people. We take work very seriously here."

Minutes pass. I try another smile but he's not playing. We sit in silence while he pretends to review the pages he's seen a million times before, turning them slowly. At last, he leans back in his chair, thrusts his hands in his tweedy jacket pockets and looks me in the eye from behind the safety of his screen. He has an irritating floppy piece of mousy hair which falls across his forehead. His eyes are startlingly blue but cold, emotionless. His lips are too big, loose and wet.

"Well Walker, you still haven't got a job I take it?" he sneers.

"Not yet," I say defensively (interpret this as *why the fuck do you think I'm here?*).

"Well, here's a chance then. I'm sending you to the Angel. Bar work, general duties. Odd hours but the pay isn't bad, considering."

Is that the hint of a smirk on his face? He takes a slip of paper out of a drawer under the counter and starts making it out, while my heart sinks even further. Does he know, I wonder, about my last bar job, and why I can't, why I won't do this one? My flustering, shy awkwardness in public until, suddenly, one day I found I had become Mr Popular, with hitherto unknown men buying me drink after drink, seeking me out for conversation? My shock and dismay at finding on the gents' toilet wall the legend: "The new barman is gay".

36

He flourishes the completed introduction slip, then pushes it under his security screen.

"I'll call the Angel to say you're coming. In about ten minutes."

Something like triumph is now playing on his face. I realise the wisdom of installing security screens in places like this. Oh, for the chance to whack a fist down on those fat fleshy fingers playing like pale tentacles on the countertop! Most of all I want this to be over, to get out and get on with the day. However round about this point I also notice something to my advantage – and I also realise that apart from Joker's initial bellow, our conversation has been kept at a low tone. J.P. Cannock's door behind my interlocutor is ajar. Had Joker kept his voice down because of this? And wait ... wasn't that the faintest sound of a radio, a portable perhaps? And did I just hear the word 'Beckham', albeit indistinctly? It couldn't be a radio tuned into the aftermath of the game, could it? Had J.P. Cannock, boss man of the Jobcentre, listened to the whole game in Japan while his minion Jones had not, a boss's perk?

It is a card I might be able to play but for a moment I keep it close to my chest.

"I'm sorry," I say, trying to make the excuse sound reasonable, "I can't do bar work. I've tried it before and I'm really hopeless at it. You'll find that I'm excused from working at bars in my notes. Mr Cannock wrote it in for me."

But there is clearly no stopping Joker now. He has scented fear perhaps.

"I'm sorry too, Walker, but I'm afraid this isn't a situation where you are in a position to refuse. I mean, I can't make you take work, but if you don't take up the offer of gainful employment, I will have to withdraw your Jobseeker's Allowance. It's as simple as that. Take it or leave it. My hands are tied. Those are the rules. Everybody has to abide by them."

He delivers this with a sort of scornful bray, and he's also turned up his volume without realising it. He ends with a shrug. No reasonableness there then! It is time for plan B – but first I can't resist getting a shot in. I lean forward, beckon him to do the same, as if I am asking him to share a confidence...

They say the place is wired, all the interviews taped, but if this is so I doubt it will pick up more than a rustle when I whisper, ironically I hope: "Thanks. That's really, *really* kind of you."

Anger knots his face instantly and he rocks back, but then I play my ace loud and clear, a calm, very reasonable voice, but nevertheless loud, as if I never cheeked him just a moment ago:

"I'm very sorry, Mr Jones, it's work I can't do in my position with a sick mother to look after. It is quite unreasonable, and I would like to see your manager. Is Mr Cannock in?"

I see from Joker's anxious sideways glance that it is spot-on to bring up the spectre of Cannock at this point. I got the pitch just right too. The radio noise ceases abruptly, a shadow falls across the crack in the door, and suddenly Cannock is standing there towering above my interrogator, tall, moustached, grey, perhaps just a little stooped but commanding, nevertheless. Joker shrinks visibly.

"A problem, Mr Jones?"

Here's a strange thing about the Jobcentre. As I said, I always seem to have a magic touch here, while so many people had bitter stories of the injustices ladled out by these small-town civil servants. For a start, I have never, ever actually been forced into anything, though Joker is by no means the first one to try. Somehow, once the reports are sifted or whatever they do with them, I am never really pushed into anything, and the old Jobseeker's Allowance, or dole by any other name, comes through good as gold. It is almost as if a guardian angel is looking after me.

"Er, no, Sir," Joker splutters deferentially (I am glad he has to call him sir). "I was just explaining there was a reasonable job offer here and Mr Walker should consider taking it. Subject to interview, of course."

Cannock looks into the distance over Joker's head, then picks up the slip which Joker has been trying to force on me. He reads it.

"Mmm. Bar work. Do you really think so, with the odd hours and all that? Mr Walker's mother really has been very ill. How is your mother, by the way?"

He turns his watery eyes on me. They are kindly, understanding.

Mum's condition has come up before here, because it really does take time and effort on my part to look after her. But I suppose I could easily take a day job, so long as it isn't far from home (and not a bar job!). Odd hours really would make things difficult. My complaint in this instance is actually justified, even if I don't relish it for an entirely different reason.

"She's still not very well Mr Cannock. Quite ill, in fact. Lots of chemotherapy."

"Oh dear, I am sorry," says Cannock, turning his watery gaze back to Joker again.

"Well, I don't think we'd better make life any more difficult for Mr Walker and his mother, do you Mr Jones?"

"No sir," Joker agrees, his voice small, downcast. I know it is a bitter pill for him to swallow. He turns to me and speaks with a lowered voice, controlled and sort of choked back.

"We'll just have to keep on looking then, shan't we Mr Walker? I think that's all we have now."

With that Cannock drifts back into his room, disappearing like a transient cloud on a hot summer's day. He has left his door ajar, however. Joker's eyes lift, venomous but impotent. He scribbles furiously and briefly in my dossier, reaches for a date stamp and slams it first on an ink pad then on a dossier page without looking up.

"That's all?"

"For now."

I stand, elated, like a player called off the subs bench. I pick up my paper and envelope, turn, and don't look back.

Luckily Roy has finished his interview too, more often than not just a rubber stamp in his case anyway, and is now in a chair near the door, waiting for me. The man still occupying the corner is snoring gently, chin on his chest, his stomach rising and falling.

"Tap?" says Roy, his eyes lighting up when he sees me. "There's something big going on at the Tap. Ballard has been talking about a wake. For England, you know. After the game."

I feel a thrill thinking about this. We emerge from the greyness and step into sunshine together. In an instant thoughts of the Jobcentre, Mum, home, and Carol Latham in the park evaporate, forgotten. The new day is waiting for us, me and Roy. The game is afoot.

Chapter 4 Opening shots

The Post Office is on our way to the Tap, so we cash our Jobseeker Giros. It's usually a good feeling. Today, because I am on a high already, it is even more superb to have a wad of crisp notes tucked in my wallet with my out-of-date provisional driving licence (I have not yet passed my test, after two abortive tries) and a photo booth picture reminding me of my brief attachment, four years ago now, to Andrea Twait.

The photo is there in case anyone asks if I have a girlfriend. Nobody does, but it is there just in case. We were both smiling, Andrea and me, when the picture was taken. I can't remember why. If I ever do show it to anyone, they might have to be told we don't see much of each other these days ... nothing at all in actual fact, Andrea being in London and for all I know married. Of course, part of her name has been mercilessly abbreviated by some people. None of this I dwell upon at this moment however, so neither does the heartburn threaten. Not immediately, anyway.

In fact, as we approach the Tap, I have a growing sense of anticipation.

The Tap wouldn't obviously be recognised by any stranger to our town as a pub, apart from King Charles being served with a pint sign above a very ordinary double doorway in the side of the Corn Exchange, an attractive four-square building of warm Bath stone. Another clue, just above ground level, is a series of extractor vents set in smoke and grime-darkened ripple glass behind stout iron grilles, normally silent in daytimes with a hint

42

of stale beer in the air but now gusting out strong wafts of warm tobacco smoke, alcohol fumes, and a loud hum of noise. A former cellar for the one-time dining rooms above, in its time it served as a Second World War bomb shelter and found its present use immediately after hostilities ceased, so they say. I doubt King Charles, who I imagine to be the jovial gent having a pint drawn from a barrel on the sign (did they have glass tankards then?), ever sipped anything in the subterranean tavern. More likely a lot of us baby-boomers were conceived in there. An oak tree depicted through the window behind the royal head is another worry. The window, not the tree. It does look rather like a double-glazed window with a uPVC frame.

"Up and down again, eh?" Roy says, grinning, referring for the millionth time to the curiosity that there are two steps up to the Tap's door followed by steep stairs going down inside, the undoing of many an unwary drinker heading in either direction. We push our way through the doors and start down the red carpeted marble flight into what can only be described as a scene of sheer bedlam.

The Tap is one big room, with a long counter at the far end and a little stage and even a mini dance floor off to the right, as you enter. Once you are inside, it could be any time of day or night. There is no way of knowing because of the darkened high-up windows. On summer evenings it's often amazing to burst out and find yourself still in daylight. Dark red upholstery, black oak woodwork and a relatively new dark green patterned carpet dubbed 'the cabbage patch' by its denizens doesn't exactly help to brighten things up. Still, it has escaped the brass, chrome and jazzy colours of fashionable modern updating and the 'Central Perk' sofas copied from the *Friends* TV show you now find in a lot of pubs. This is perhaps why its retro air is popular not only with the students attending the tall 1950s concrete and glass fledgling university across the road, but also with many other young people in the town anxious to be seen as nonconformist. There's that, and the fact it serves pints for a pound, which the classier places don't. It is connected with the local brewery, Hopcraft Ales, their brews inconsistent in strength and quality yet occasionally lethal enough to genetically modify entire generations.

Entering the noise barrier today is like having to force ourselves through a solid brick wall. At the back of the stage is the biggest television screen I have ever seen, while from the opposite end of the room the resident juke box is also going full blast, wanging out an incomprehensible and jerky hip-hop number. These rival electronics appear to be having a competition for which can be the loudest, while the heaving, *really* heaving, floor space and tables are packed with jabbering people. It is hot as hell, and despite the extractors going full blast smoke hangs visibly in a thick blue layer just above people's heads. Instant slipstream cancer.

Whoever controls the giant screen is constantly channel hopping, settling momentarily only when it displays some part of that morning's football game or a reference to it. Roy nudges me and points in this direction as we reach the bottom, feeling rather like aircraft, a rather clonky aircraft in Roy's case, dropping out of the clouds and coming in to land. Clouds noticeably laced with wandering strands of cannabis smoke, I might add.

"Glory be, look at that!" There is awe in Roy's voice. He is looking at the dance floor space in front of the screen.

While a giant Beckham is taking a corner behind her, a shoeless woman in a tight fitting bright red dress is dancing. There is no discernible reference to the juke box rhythm in her gyrations.

She also seems to be having some trouble with her bra, fiddling around inside the top of her clothes. But then to my complete astonishment she suddenly withdraws the unhooked lacy black undergarment and waves it in the air with triumph and tosses it aside into the crowd with a flourish. Hands grasp in the air for it and the bra vanishes. A ragged cheer breaks out from nearby tables, but then a hush falls. She has started rolling up the frilly hem of her dress towards her waist.

I am quite shocked because it is Glynnis Cannock. Glynnis, the most desirable girl in town, the girl the boys, in my generation, anyway, would most like to be with. Glynnis the unattainable, for she is 'Dicker' Jones' girl, or so it is said. She is also daughter of the Jobcentre boss who has so recently released me from an unpleasant trap set by Dicker's brother.

As I watch, even more astonished, she tugs at the bottom hem of her knickers, starts inching them down while she shimmies to the music no-one else can hear.

Two girlfriends appear at her side. They are considerably more sober than she is. They are trying to get her to stop the impromptu striptease, but she pushes them away, tosses her shiny black hair and carries on with the floor show. The knickers come off while she wobbles first on one leg, then the other, and then they follow the bra through the air and into the cheering crowd. At this the friends reappear, grabbing an arm apiece. To a chorus of boos they wrestle her offstage. That, it appears, is as far as they are going to let her go.

I feel Roy nudging me. I have fallen into a gawping daze. Snapping myself out of it, we set off for the bar.

"She'll be sorry tomorrow morning," says Roy.

You see? The Tap effect. Already he has forgotten the time of day and is clearly thinking it is evening.

Roy is happy to trail behind me across the crowded floor, dragging his plastered leg, miraculously avoiding almost certain further damage in the press of bodies. On the way I step in something soft. Looking down (not altogether easy in the crush) I see half a bacon bap is stuck to the sole of one of my trainers. I shake it off, but a few steps on I feel the crunch of broken glass underfoot. There are now more cheers from the direction of the stage, but in the crush at the bar I can't quite see what is going on.

The overalled slavies behind the counter are very busy. They all have glistening red faces and the glazed look of people working on automatic pilot under pressure, but one small fair round-faced youth has finished handing someone change. Feeling luck is with me I shout an order for a couple of pints of ordinary.

"Two. Cat's-piss."

"Four," Roy corrects at my elbow. He winks conspiratorially. "Couple each, eh? Save coming back soon."

But another voice cuts in before I can change the order: Mick Shoebury, the Tap manager, bow-tied for the occasion, has appeared in the sometimes-shadowy way he does beside his barman.

"Hello Pete. I'll get those," he says, smiling at me, and aside to the bar boy: "Ring two pints up to me, will you?" He turns

46

back to me before gliding on, too fast for a reply, and says: "Bad luck about the game, eh? Mum all right? I hope she is..."

And he's gone again leaving me with a barely uttered "Thanks..." on my lips.

On quiet days in the Tap, and there are sometimes quiet times, Mick, wispy hair glued from side to side across his shiny and ever-growing bald patch, would take a great deal of time and trouble to tell us that pop music today wasn't worth a fig compared to the sixties. He had played in a band himself, therefore he knew. You had to be there, they say.

"Two more," I say to the bar boy as we down the free ones quickly.

We start to drink these too while we still hold a beachhead at the counter. I can drink quickly. Then I get in another one each and Roy insists on getting us another one each too before we strike out, with already a sort of swishy feeling going on in my stomach, glasses in each hand, to where the level of noise indicates the centre of attention. It is also the direction in which we last saw Glynnis Cannock.

But the show is over. A dazed Glynnis, minus shoes as well as presumably knickers and bra, is being comforted by the two friends at the side of the giant screen. They are having some trouble keeping her upright. By now her main audience during the striptease, a group of fifteen or so packed round three largish tables pushed together to the side of the stage, has turned its attention elsewhere. We manage to find the barest room to squeeze onto the bench seat at the edge of the crowd, me going in first, with our backs to the wall and just out of sight of the TV screen.

The group is in what you might call a state of flux. People are breaking away in ones and twos while others join. After just a few moments it seems as if the whole pub is a hive and this is its social epicentre, the royal cell. The focus of the group itself is clear to see, or rather more noticeably hear – the redoubtable Quentin Ballard, a very opinionated queen bee in his cups, sitting opposite us across the composite of crowded tables.

"I tell you," he is saying, "that bloke Beckham is ignorant. Dead ignorant. And as for Posh Spice ... posh? She's as ignorant as he is..."

Somebody further along the wall stands up to leave. He pushes past me and Roy to get out, and we edge up a space, nearer the earthquake zone. That gives us room to put our drinks down in a sea of glasses. By now the Cat's Piss is going down nicely and we have started on the last ones. I look up to find Ballard's wild black eyes have lighted on me, temporarily I hope.

"S'right, isn't it - ask young Walker there. They all take the piss out of Posh because she's dead ignorant, isn't she?"

Faces turn towards me. Embarrassed, I start to open my mouth to reply, but there is more to come from the leering Ballard and my voice sticks in my throat.

"So's Walker, though ... all he knows about is Andrea's twat. Isn't that right?" He looks round for approval. Oh no – not the Angela Twait thing again. I groan inwardly, try to make myself unnoticeable.

Ballard's jibe earns a collective guffaw. But mercifully for me he moves on. He is still in full flow, but the heat is off me. I swallow a surge of rising acid. We do feel truly part of the group now, though, after that introduction. Quentin Ballard is much older than he looks. He is nearer Mum's age, but he's always with this younger group. Some a good deal younger than me, when I think of it, and a certain clique look up to him with almost adoration. A reporter with the *Argus*, he has a sort of Quixotic appeal. He's larger than life, that's for sure, and pretty noisy when he's holding court. He led a wild youth, according to many accounts, roaming the world in the age of the hippy until returning here, to his home town. Settling down would be the wrong words for Ballard though.

Among many dark and unconfirmed rumours, always delivered in a hushed voice, is one that he murdered someone in some desperate foreign escapade. To hear him you'd say he was a bit of a toff though, much more so than Posh Spice. Anyone called Quentin must be posh, after all. As I say, he doesn't look anything like his age. He still has long curly blond hair for a start, falling away from a central parting, and he doesn't look, as some people do, like someone trying to hold onto their looks too long. Fashionable clothes and half glasses help this effect and while he is pontificating like now (which is often) he talks looking over the rim. Another rumour is he regularly knocks off the younger women among the adoring acolytes. Some blokes look up to him too. Others are jealous. I think I might be one of those, a bit. Some almost spit when they hear his name.

Among other notables in the Tap top-table group are Martin Throgmore, nicknamed Toad, a perpetual student even though he is a bit older than me; Gerry Powell, optician's assistant by day and rake and man about town in the evening; a strikingly pretty girl with waist-length curly red-gold hair who I have never heard say anything and whose name I didn't know. She's always around town though, day and night, often with a sand-coloured whippet lurcher on a string and a haversack on her back, as if they are setting off somewhere; sharp-witted and bespectacled Becky Jackson, another contemporary of mine who I quite like, and the notorious Dicker Jones, who at this moment is slumped forward asleep on the table between Toad and Gerry Powell. Is this why Glynnis is in such a state, I wonder?

"Look!" hisses Roy, nodding towards the copper-blonde street nomad, "It's Goldilocks." This is her nickname, though not to her face so far as I know.

I watch Ballard warily. He has paused for a pull on a joint which has reached him on its way round the table. At the other end of the group from us one of the art students is busily crafting another, a monster, absorbed in pasting many cigarette papers together in an elaborate pattern.

Somebody pushes in on the other side of Roy and for the moment we are locked in the group dynamic, with my unfashionably brick-like phone now pressed even tighter up to a large-bottomed girl on my other side who has her elbows on the table, chin propped in her hands, and is gazing adoringly at Ballard. I've seen the girl before. 'Thunderthighs' is an unkind nickname someone has given her. For once I don't feel too embarrassed and there is a cosy oneness about everything.

Ballard exhales his held-back marijuana smoke in a noisy gasp and the already-blanketing air around our party becomes even thicker.

"So," he says, leaning forward. "It's a wake then, is it, in the Park? About six. A wake in the park ... no, wait for it, a wake by the lake, in the park in the dark."

He looks round at his audience with triumph. However, most of them are too far gone to recognise pot-inspired doggerel. Then a slurred voice rang out.

"Won't be dark, though, will it."

There is a sort of shudder in the group. Who had dared to question the master word-tosser? All eyes turn on Martin Throgmore.

The shadow of a frown passes over Ballard's face. Then he smiles.

"Toad my friend, my dear, dear Toad, you are of course right, as always. But not very poetic, perhaps," he says, gesturing with an airy wave in the air, then closing his fist and whacking it on the table.

"But that won't matter, will it? We'll all meet here around four, pour in the door, get pissed till we list and parade to a glade in the shade for a wake by the lake in the park ... light or dark ..."

"The cops won't let us." Throgmore says in a world-weary voice.

This time Ballard draws himself up straight to meet the challenge.

"Cops?" he says with heavy scorn. "Cops? Do any of you know how many cops there are in town at this very moment? Well, I'll tell you, and trust me, for I assuredly am a chief constable. There is one policeman, one rather nervous bloke who would rather not be a policeman in a flack jacket who's been told to be a presence in the Square all day. All his mates have been despatched to be presences in the towns and villages of this noble shire on this memorable day in our history, this momentous event which has brought our proud nation to its

51

knees, just as it brought the honourable Captain Beckham to his knees, because the boozers have been open since dawn and there might be a bit of bovver."

For a moment there is silence round the group, even Throgmore.

"Way to go, Balsy!" Thunderthighs shouts out suddenly beside me, gazing at Ballard with obvious admiration. "Smackimdown, the fuckin' killjoy!"

She turns to me, a leer on her face, looking for affirmation. I can't think of anything to say and turn away.

"Good," says Ballard relaxing. He gives another little smile, directed I imagine especially at the silenced Throgmore. "Here at four, in the door, out at six, off to the sticks, into the park ... light or dark." Then louder, "For Chrissake lighten up everyone, this is a wake! We party!"

At that moment another kerfuffle at the opposite end of the table draws everyone's attention: Glynnis Cannock, still decidedly the worst for wear, is trying to push herself in between the sitters and the tables, making everyone stand in turn to make way. Her companions have vanished, and she is presumably wearing no more now than when she had finished her dance, apart from a minute shiny red bag which doesn't look as if it will hold anything worth carrying. Her progress is slow, glasses full or empty tumbling as she passes, but by degrees she gets to Thunderthighs next to me, who tut-tuts at having to rise. Me next. Is she going right through? But after negotiating Thunderthighs Glynnis lands herself with a thump on her bottom on the bench at my side, wedging herself between me and the glaring heavyweight. The disturbance this causes passes back along the row like shunted train wagons.

"Thish my drink?" Glynnis clutches my remaining pint and gazes at me squiffilly. She raises it unsteadily and takes a long pull. "S'better." She puts the glass down and wipes her mouth with the back of her hand. Putting the bag on the table, she slumps back. "Sh'Pete, ishn' it? Pete Walker?"

A sudden silence falls over everything. Perhaps, though, I am just unaware of anything else for the moment except me and her.

Fingers clutch my arm.

"Whoa!" she says. "Stopitall moving."

She lets go of me, hitches her scarlet dress so far up I can very nearly see the knickerless tops of her legs, puts her head between her knees and is noiselessly sick on the floor.

"Shit!" exclaims Thunderthighs, wrinkling her nose and edging away.

"Shorry," Glynnis says to me, not to Thunderthighs. She is sitting up, legs apart, looking down, aghast at the sour-smelling pool she has deposited.

"Here," I say quickly, and not quite knowing why I think it would be a good idea I unfold the Argus World Cup Special wrap-around that I have stuffed in my pocket and help her arrange it over the mess.

"Shorry," she says again, rolling down her dress and stretching her legs under the table so that the torn and kneeling Beckham's new-found extra indignity is hidden, and with that she leans back again. Her head falls lightly on my shoulder. At the same time her hot sticky hand reaches out and finds mine, squeezes it and holds on. In less than a minute she is asleep,

53

mouth slightly open, leaving me acutely aware I am pressed against a woman virtually naked apart from a skimpy tube of fabric, with only my mobile phone keeping us apart.

Mixed panic and sheer elation sweep over me, a feeling far beyond anything I have ever known before. I don't want to move, change anything.

When I do look up, I know for sure the whole group has been watching this charade in complete silence. But people look away immediately, nobody meets my eyes, and they seem to all at once find other interesting things to say to neighbours. I shoot an anxious look towards Dicker, Glynnis's boyfriend, but he remains slumped, not a movement, dead to the world in general and unaware of her apparent unfaithfulness. And the hubbub gradually increases again.

I am jarred out of wondering what the hell to do in this new situation by a jab in the ribs from the other side. I have all but forgotten Roy. And although I am scared the movement might wake Glynnis, I turn to see he is looking at me with some admiration.

"I'll get us another drink," he says. "D'you think she wants one too?"

I signal 'no' with a wave of my spare hand, not daring to shake my head and wake this sleeping angel who has sought my protection.

He goes. I expect him back shortly, but I don't see him reappear. Perhaps he has been trampled in the crowd. Heaven knows what could happen with his advanced level of vulnerability. He just slips silently and swiftly out of my racing mind.

Two things happen almost together after that.

First, Ballard's mobile phone rings – he is called away.

"The edition waits on my word," he announces to the group which has hushed to overhear his phone conversation. "The mighty presses rest for no man, or woman. Adieu! We meet again here at four, conspirators. We meet to weep for Beckham, for Sven, for England, Harry and St George!"

The other thing is a PA announcement that the Tap is shutting temporarily to clear up but will reopen again at 1pm. The group immediately starts to break up, tables noisily pushed out of the way. The party is clearly over ... this stage of it anyway.

Now I must act. I shake Glynnis gently. I am scared she either will not wake at all or will react violently towards me when she realises who she is with. We scarcely know each other, do we?

Neither of those things happens. Instead, she opens her eyes and smiles. Though a bit red round the rims, her eyes are dark and deep.

"I feel like shit," she says, letting me help her to her feet. "D'you think you can get me home?"

An irrelevance pops into my head. I still have not had my football conversation. At this moment it does not seem so important.

From the corner of my eye I see Dicker is being helped towards the steps ahead of us, suspended between Gerry Powell on one side and another bloke I don't know. I don't hurry towards the steps with Glynnis.

Chapter 5 Opportunity knocks

We do not have to hunt around much in the surrounding debris to find the red shoes that went with her dress and bag. Fortunately, we don't bother looking for the rest of her discarded things. The Tap's staff are teetering round us over the crunchy and slippery floor collecting dangerously tall stacks of dirty glasses.

Not many times in my life have I felt a victim to odd circumstances, yet as I eventually guide Glynnis up the steps of the Tap, her half leaning for support and half companionably arm in arm, matters are definitely a long way out of my control.

"Steady," I caution as we negotiate the trick up-and-down steps at the top (I have had a few myself, remember). This means her holding on to me quite tightly, and as we step blinking into the sunlight, I can't help feeling in charge of her, responsible. The funny notion strikes me, not for the first time today, and not with the same person, that we could to all intents and purposes be seen as partners, she and I. At least it might seem that way to onlookers. I expect the couple in the park who earlier saw me with Carol Latham and her baby, should they happen to pass at this moment, would be surprised I am so fickle. There aren't any onlookers though. Just one nervous flack-jacketed policeman, as Ballard predicted, on the corner of the Square. He is indeed completely alone and is either talking into his walkie-talkie thing or a mobile phone or whatever policemen carry or is making a pretence of doing so. The instrument is even more brick-like and unfashionable than mine. He is one of the few Asian policemen we have on the local force.

Dicker and his companions have vanished. I'm very glad of that.

"Thanks," says Glynnis at the kerb. We pause and gulp some fresh air.

I try to reply casually: "S'all right."

I am surprised at the deep sound of my own voice, and proud that she still holds on to me because she really isn't as pissed now as she had been in the pub. I start muttering about taxis, but she nudges me, and this sets us both moving forward on our feet. Sensible in this taxi-arid town. We head out across the Square, right under the copper's nose.

"This way."

She now sounds stronger. We go down narrow Sheep Street, newly fake-cobbled and pedestrianised, and towards the slightly ghettoised part of town where students' lodgings, bedsits and cheap flats abound.

"A shithole, this bloody town, don't you think?" she says suddenly. "I've got to get out of it. What about you?"

The question takes me aback. Somewhere in there sounded as if it might be a sort of invitation. But I can't always think quickly, and this was one of those occasions when I couldn't find an apt response.

"The town? Yes, it is a bit of a dump," I agree, tailing off and wondering how else I might react.

"You can't like it, can you? Dead. There's nothing here," she continues, frowning at the ground ahead.

Her arm slips out of mine, but our hands brush and her fingers catch at mine, hold on, warm and moist. She is still leading me, now more purposefully.

"Up here."

We enter a street of terrace houses much like my home street, but the road is narrower, and without trees. After a little way she edges me towards a gateway with a tiny overgrown weedy front garden leading up to the porch. It is a house not unlike ours, the same style, same period, but divided into two flats, I can see from the bell pushes. She gets the key in the lock after a couple of attempts and shoves the door open scattering a pile of mail. Mostly junk I would say. She catches my hand again and she doesn't let go of me as we climb a flight of stairs, open another door. Inside, I'm tugged quickly cross an untidy living room-cum-kitchen to another open door and ... a bedroom. It is smaller than my bedroom and almost filled by an unmade single bed. Here at last she lets go of my hand. She sits down on side of the bed and turns her face up at me.

"Christ, I really do feel awful."

She looks it. Then her expression changes, as if she has suddenly thought of something, and she twists round to tip the contents of her bag on the top of a bedside cupboard.

"Wait, give me a minute..."

One of the things that falls out is a dinky mobile phone with a bright cover, blue with orange stars. She picks it up, switches it on and frowns as a message alert sounds. She listens, the frown deepening, then switches the thing off and slams it down, bad tempered.

"Bastard!" she says suddenly and vehemently. Then, quieter, tired: "Sorry. I don't really know what's going on. Are you going back to the Tap tonight? The wake?"

"Probably."

"Mmm. Might see you there."

And with that she kicks off her red shoes, rolls herself onto the bed face down, stretches out full length, and falls silent.

I stand for fully two minutes before I realise she has passed out.

I am alone again, or I might as well be. Alone with a near-naked woman, skimpy red dress rucked up and revealing on one side a bare and wonderfully plump rounded buttock.

Staring open-mouthed I feel suddenly ashamed. I locate the loose corner of her duvet and pull it over her. When she still does not stir I look around, acutely aware that I should not stay here.

Among the other things that have fallen from that tiny bag of hers, I notice, are some folded tenners and loose change, and an unopened condom packet. I tiptoe out, leaving her snoring.

Not much chance there of having a conversation about the game, or anything else. If there ever had been anything else.

Out in the street again it occurs to me it might be getting on a bit, the time, and it is. It's nearly a quarter to one! Where did the intervening hours go?

Tempted as I am to dawdle and muse over the quite extraordinary day so far, I set off at a pace, thinking now of mum and her lunch needs. I thread my way back to the town centre. I pass through it and set a line for home to take me past Stenton's the butcher.

Roger Stenton is ready for me when a small queue in front has been dealt with by him and his spotty assistant, a boy who can never speak without blushing deeply. I sympathise with the tongue-tied sixteen-year-old.

"Couple of chops ... like mum likes them?" the butcher asks. "Tell you what, I'll do four."

All I must do is nod and pay up when they have been cut, trimmed with what is always some degree of care and a bit of showmanship, and wrapped.

"No - thank *you*," Stenton says in reply to my thanks. He is a handsome, dark-haired man but growing jowly, like people who eat a lot of meat often do. "Give mum my best wishes, eh? And tell her to get well soon." And he adds for the benefit of the customers now building up behind, because he fancies himself a bit of a comedian: "Hey, if Beckham and his boys had eaten British chops like that before the game instead of sushi-wooshi, we'd have sent those Brazilians packing for sure. Like we did the Krauts."

It raises a titter or two. No price has been mentioned. He hands me what I think is rather a lot of change from my fiver.

Outside the shop I run straight into Carol, coming towards me and still pushing Toby.

"Hi!" I give her a friendly smile.

But she scowls. Is she cross? Why? I make to go on past, but the pushchair slews round to bar my way. This leaves the fatherless Toby staring in a bemused way at the wheels of passing cars.

"I heard you was in the Tap."

She is hot and bothered about something.

"Er, yes," I agree. I am not quite sure what is going on. But I am something to do with her flapping, there is no doubt. I don't have a clue what it is except it is something to do with my visit to the Tap.

"You going with that Glynnis Cannock?" she suddenly blurts out.

So that's it, a straight accusation. There are things in the wind of which I have no perception. The small-town rumour-mill has clearly worked fast and worked well.

"No."

I speak cautiously, and so far as I know at this stage quite truthfully, naively uncertain where all this is leading. She looks marginally relieved.

"I helped her home though. She was pissed."

"Oh, she was, was she."

"She was. Well pissed. Passed out."

There is silence, then she starts to unfreeze a bit. She pulls Toby partly out of my path, a bit roughly I think, and gives a little smile.

"There's a big party going on in the park tonight, I heard?"

"I think so. Ballard's set up something."

"You going?"

"I might," I say. "Depends on Mum."

"I'm going. I'm getting our mum to sit again," she says. "See you there?"

61

More of an appeal than a statement, I feel.

I try to act cool, be cautious. "Could be," I say, and start moving. As I edge past, she flashes her warmer park smile again.

"Seeyah!" she says to my back. I don't look back, but I can feel she is watching until I turn the corner.

Soon I'm passing Singh's and musing on the strangeness of women. There is no sign of my Indian tormenters. A shame, because at this moment I feel I could cope better with the horrid little harpies than any time in my life before.

I am still thinking along these lines as I turn into our street. Even as I round the corner, I know something bad is up. The brick house frontages around me are flashing on and off, reflecting a pulsating blue light. I stop in my tracks. There is an ambulance outside our house.

***

My heart throttles up into overdrive. I start to run: The vehicle is facing away from me, and I can see that the engine is running, with a thin plume of blue smoke coming from the exhaust pipe. But even as I get closer, with still a hundred or so yards to go, a green-suited paramedic steps briskly out of our front door, makes his way round to the driver's side of the vehicle and hops in, shutting the door. The ambulance starts to move off immediately. The flashing blue light goes out. Jesus, what does that mean? Am I too late?

"Wait!" I shout as loudly as I can, being out of breath.

By now I am running like hell. However, the van gathers speed and is leaving the end of the street before I reach our gate. I stop and stand watching it disappear, holding onto the gatepost.

When I get my breath back a bit, I notice there is a car parked a little forward of the gate. It looks like our doctor's car.

Now I'm worried sick. The front door is ajar, and I also see that a pane of glass near the door handle is broken, with most of the glass shards removed. I push it open and go in.

***

She is still there, of course, sitting up and looking perky as you like.

"I pushed the panic button, Petey," she says, flashing one of her smiles. "Such drama! My oh my."

"Christ, mum!" I am in a cold sweat. "What happened?"

"Just a little hiccup. A flutter."

She titters, quite unlike her, and manages to look like a naughty little girl who won't own up to stealing the cake she is hiding behind her back, or someone who has just helped a younger sibling to tip over the edge of the cot. She has probably been given something, morphine perhaps. Then I hear the sound of the loo door, and someone walking along the passage.

"Is that the doctor?"

It is Doctor Cohen, Simon Cohen, thankfully not the youngest medic in the practice, Paul Jenkins, a man I don't think she entirely trusts. Doctor Cohen though has an air of mature authority but manages to come over as friendly rather than aloof.

"Ah," he says coming into the room. "You're here. Good. Mum had a little scare. I think we've got it under control."

He is a handsome young man, I guess, although short. He could be a magazine doctor, or one of the medics in a hospital soap opera. He is smartly dressed in a waistcoat and tweed suit

63

trousers which are not his working clothes. Probably he has been called away from some function. He has just washed his hands in the loo and is drying them on a tissue handkerchief, not trusting the cleanliness of our towels, perhaps. He puts the crumpled-up paper on the table beside Mum and begins to stow instruments away in his black bag. When he has finished, he snaps it shut.

To my annoyance Mum is looking at him with undisguised admiration, the way she does sometimes with certain men. That embarrasses me too. Come to think of it, it is quite easy to embarrass me, and not just mum that does it. It goes along with the general feeling I have that there is something wrong with me, abnormal. Perhaps it is something to do with virginity, that sort of thing. That can't be normal at my age, can it?

"Just one last check," Dr Cohen says, reaching for her hand lying outside the covers. He takes her wrist, feels for a pulse.

"Am I still alive?" Mum says, mocking but still clearly in a state of worship.

"Just about.

He grins at me.

"We must take more care of Mum," he says.

I thought: *Oh, she's your mum too, is she?*

"Tch!" says Mum, suddenly irritated. "It's not Peter's fault. He can't always be here. He's a young man. He's got his own life to lead."

"Of course," Dr Cohen says, still looking at me. "Did you see the game this morning?"

"We both did, Mum and me," I said. "We watched it together."

"Bad luck England, eh?" he continues. "Still, I suppose we were lucky to get that far anyway. I thought it was a very creditable effort though, didn't you? They might have run all over us. Beckham did a good job."

"Nice boy!" Mum butts in. She is beginning to get tetchy, her admiration for the doctor fading. Maybe she is miffed at being left out of this outbreak of boys' talk. She wants to be the centre of attention again. He doesn't seem to notice her interruption.

She probably doesn't like that either. It reinforces some of her 'it's a man's world' theories.

"Seaman really did his best, I think," the doctor says, still recalling he game. "Nasty fall, though. It would set him back, despite the raised adrenaline level – that helps you rise above pain. Lucky it wasn't more serious. As a doctor, I would have had to advise against playing on, just to be safe. Probably lucky I'm not a sports doctor."

Encouraged by all this I find my tongue and start to launch into my long-dormant game conversation. At last, an enthusiast...

"Right from the kick off..." I begin.

"Yes, yes," he agrees, but with it comes a little frown which could be read as annoyance. Is he wasting time? He picks his jacket off the back of a dining chair and starts to pull it on. Then he edges towards the door. This is clearly not the moment to open the subject out.

He speaks again, briskly: "Lots of match autopsies going on everywhere now. Look, I'm a bit late for something. Can you bring my bag out to the car Peter? Bye bye, Mrs Walker. Please take care. We'll have you back to rights soon, I'm sure."

My game conversation has hit the rocks again.

He goes through the door before I can say any more. I pick up his bag, surprisingly heavy, and follow him out.

At the gate he stops, turns and takes the bag from me. His manner has changed again and now he is looking deadly serious. This takes some moments to register because I am still in a rather far-gone state, I discover in the fresh air. Drinking before lunch is maybe not a very good idea. You only must do it to realise why.

"Right, Peter. I didn't want to speak with your mum listening. You're doing a grand job looking after her, but she has to have a proper downstairs bed, more care. We seem to be moving into a, er, well, a different phase. I know you're a responsible carer, but would you like me to contact Social Services for you? Get extra help?"

I sober suddenly. "Is she worse?"

He looks first at the sky, then back at my shoulder.

"Hard to say. It could just be a bad day."

"That's what she said this morning. She said it was different," I tell him. The morning seems a long while ago.

"I see. Well, time will tell."

He is suddenly brisk again, going to the car and opening it and talking over his shoulder as he throws the bag across to the passenger seat.

"Call me straightaway if there are any more problems."

"I will."

He starts the engine and draws away in one movement, waving a salute out of the window.

When I get back Mum has drawn herself up to sit. She has more colour, I am glad to see.

"Well, doc, level with me," she mocks. "You were gone a long time. What did he say to you? Call the priest?"

"Just football talk, that's all. How do you feel? What happened?"

I look at the call alarm system the district nurse left with her some time back. She has a thingy on a cord round her neck connected with some apparatus by the phone, and she just has to press a button if she's in trouble.

"Did you use that?" I pointed.

"I don't know what happened. I just found myself on the floor. And so cold. Yes, I used it, must have done. Works pretty good, doesn't it?"

"Be serious, Mum. Are you all right?"

She shrugs and the corners of her mouth turn down.

"I don't know. I think so. I mean, it's gone, whatever it was, and I'm no worse than I was this morning. You've been drinking a bit, haven't you?"

This is clearly as serious as she is going to get for now.

"You know I was going to the Tap, don't you? I'll get our chops done. You can eat some, can't you?"

Her eyes widen.

"From Roger?"

This might be the first time she said just 'Roger' without his surname.

"Yes."

"Did he say anything?"

"He asked after you. And I said you were OK. He said get well soon."

"I wish," She nods. "Good."

I cook the chops with sliced onions and fry some cold potato from the fridge to go with them. I also heat some canned peas, make Bisto gravy. I carry in two platefuls plus a cup of tea each. Her appetite is obviously back, and she eats it all without pause, though she complains everything tastes much too salty, especially the Bisto. I disagree. She says it must be the medicine that makes it taste like that then.

While we eat – I'm really hungry too – I tell her about my day so far. Bits of it, anyway, including what Ballard said and the planned wake. She looks up when she hears his name. I can't remember if he has ever come up in conversations between us before. When I finish the narrative, she is looking serious.

"How come you know Quentin Ballard?" she says. "I'd have thought he was rather out of your age group."

I tell her what I know about the company Ballard keeps and repeat some of the less-lurid rumours about him and women. She smiles.

"The old bugger," she says with a little snort. "A dirty old man at last. I always though he would be."

"You know him?"

I believe she is blushing, though it is hard to tell this in the subdued light of the room. There is a silence. When she speaks again, she is steering away from the subject.

"You know, Peter, you really must get out more. Especially get out of this pokey little town, see the world, get some experience, do things. It's a hole. And full of creeps, no-hopers."

"You're the second person to say that to me today," I say, adding, "Well, sort of."

It is my turn to blush when I think of Glynnis.

"Good. Then perhaps you will. You don't have to wait for me to push off, you know. Our gallant Social Services team will step in and speed me on my way, no doubt. You could go tomorrow. People do clear out, just like that. I mean it."

"Mum," I complain, "Stop. I'm not leaving you. Not ... like this."

"No, I will *not* stop. And if you've got an offer from someone to go with, take it up. Vanish. I would, like a shot. It is a girl, I assume. You're not gay, are you? I don't mind if you are, really. Might as well tell me. I could help you if you are."

"Mum!"

Protesting too much? I find myself facing *that* question again, as I had done before, remembering how I was shocked by the attention of the men in my one and only bar job, and how the thought of what men did with men filled me with revulsion. But then if you've never had the experience, just how do you know? Could I be, deep down? Is that the reason I'm still a virgin? Anguish! Christ, do these things stay with you? I mean, when I'm in my thirties and forties, with a wife and children and all, as I sometimes imagine I will be, will I still be having these stabs of anguish?

I drag my mind away from the thought and having hidden the fact that I have embarrassed myself completely with the gay issue, I tell her about Glynnis. Well, most of it. But I leave out her name.

"Mmm, go for it Petey. You don't get an offer like that every day. Is she a looker?"

"Stop," I complain again, and she giggles to see my embarrassment.

"Sorry," she says. "But I really think you're a bit ... well, slow, sometimes. You *are* seeing her again?"

"Maybe, at this wake thing later. Only perhaps I shouldn't go out again now, not with you like this."

"Like what?"

"Well ... unwell." The contradiction in these two words suddenly strikes me as funny.

"I'm fine now Pete. Look, absolutely right as rain, sound as a pound." She raises a clenched fist in a black power salute, as if this proves she has recovered. "You must go. Follow through, my boy."

"I'll see." I shrug and clear up, take things to the kitchen to wash-up.

"I should have given you a father," she shouts after me. "He'd tell you what to do. I'm sorry I can't."

"Tell me what?" I shout back, all ears, but she has nothing more to say on the subject it seems. She and I have never got very far with talking about my provenance. At first, when I was much younger, she would say I didn't need a dad when there was her and Gran to look after me. That was true enough at the time. Later, in the company of people who mostly did have fathers, it seemed quite reasonable to ask again. I did so several

70

times. She gave two answers to this beyond which we did not travel: the first and most frequent was that it did not matter who he was, and it would make no difference to my life now that I was growing up, and the second (in more recent times) was that she did not actually know for sure. The first answer gave the most hope that he might be identifiable, the second made me scrutinise all men of a certain age for similarities in my own make up that might put the finger on the 'suspect'. From time to time I tried to imagine him, the figure emerging in my imagination being a composite of rather a lot of people. Cannock, for example, was one of them, Roger Stenton another, Mick Shoebury too ... and now, for the first time, there was Ballard to consider, seeing how Mum knew him as well...

I realise there is another side to all this too: somebody out there must have at least an inkling he has sired a son, even if he seems reluctant to take up the responsibilities. Again, there are from time to time those little unexpected kindnesses that come my way as they have done today: a free beer, good value at the butcher's counter, an easy ride at the Jobcentre.

I come back after washing-up wondering if this might at last be a good opportunity to reopen the paternity debate again. I find she has settled herself back down and is fast asleep. Yes, I think, *you should have given me a father*.

I creep upstairs and kick my boots off, lie on my bed and shut my eyes, ready for a short nap.

When I wake, sweating heavily, it is already four o'clock, which is the time Ballard decreed the the World Cup Wake ought to start.

Chapter 6 Dark revelations

As I come round from my extremely feverish sleep, the memory of a vivid dream is still fresh in my head. I had been hand in hand with Glynnis in a beautiful spot beside a little river, just standing and looking at each other's faces in a soppy way, when a shout made us look up. A man with a huge butcher's meat cleaver was glaring at us angrily from a ridge top. He looked very much like Roger Stenton.

He started coming towards us, raging. Then there was another shout from the other direction, and I looked up at the other side of the valley to see David Beckham and most of the England football team, who also loooked extremely angry. Don't ask me why, there was no apparent reason. I started to run downstream with Glynnis, and the valley began to look very familiar. At this point I realised, without a shade of embarrassment, I was wearing nothing but my underpants while Glynnis had only her clinging skimpy red dress. Suddenly Carol, wearing no top at all, just jeans, appeared paddling a large log in mid-stream. She beckoned. It seemed clear that to escape our pursuers we would have to ride with her. We plunged in, struck out for the log and scrambled aboard. Now there was me in the middle holding onto Carol's waist, while Glynnis's arms wrapped around me from behind. This felt all rather grand and believe me very sexy. Not only were we travelling so fast that we were sure to escape, but whenever Carol turned around, she looked happy. And when I then looked round at Glynnis she too was grinning. And I was pressed between both of them ...

We came rushing round a bend and then, suddenly, there was a bridge ahead of us. It was the bridge of my picture, only as we raced closer it began changing into a tunnel, long, narrow and low ... and at this point I woke up. With an erection.

And I hear Mum coughing again.

I go down to make sure she is all right. She seems to be fine. However, there's certainly no time now for raising the paternity issue if I want to make the wake, so I go back up to take off my sweaty clothes and have a quick wash with a hot flannel. I then put out some smart clothes but suddenly remember the eventual destination is the park, in the dark. So, I put the clean shirt, jeans and jumper back in their drawers and instead I settle for my other pair of jeans and the thick polo-neck sweater I usually only like wearing around home.

Then I go downstairs again and make some tea. Mum watches in silence as I get the teapot, cups and milk together and bring them over to her.

"Good. You're going out."

I help her to lay out her evening array of pills then go to the kitchen to make cheese and tomato sandwiches which I put on a plate beside her covered with a tea towel. She needs a big bottle of still spring water and a glass in reach too, to wash it all down, and I see to this quickly.

"You are sure you'll be all right?" I say when all her essentials are set up.

"I'm fine. But you should eat something too. Promise me. You can't just go on drinking alcohol. You'll make yourself ill."

"I will eat, Mum," I promise. "But I'll come back early, eh?"

"Whatever. But I don't think I'd leave the party early, not if I were you. What do you think is going to happen to me? I've got my alarm next to me, look. And we know it works now, don't we?" She dangles the device in the air on its cord.

I go out to grab a pork pie I know is in the fridge, and I must admit at this stage I am quite looking forward to getting out. I'm also relieved now about Mum's welfare, seeing how well she seems. She looks quite good, much better than when I came in.

"And what's this girl's name?" she asks, louder, before I come out of the kitchen.

"Glynnis," I tell her. "Glynnis Cannock. She's quite posh. Her dad's the boss at the Jobcentre."

There's no reply, but there is a small sound. Precursor to a cough? However, when I come back into the room everything as calm. She has spilled a little tea on her blanket, though, and I help her mop it up.

I slip on my jacket, patting my pocket to make sure my wallet is still there.

"Look," she says, just as I am leaving. This time she is graver. "Don't take your old Mum's matchmaking pleas too seriously, eh? Play the field. There's plenty of choice out there, especially for a nice boy like you."

Embarrassed again, I put the television control by her hand, kiss her on the cheek. Without looking back, I head for the door.
***

It was fun growing up with Mum and Gran, especially before the age when I began to realise not everyone else was like us, and there were people with brothers and sisters out there. And fathers. And standard families were the preferred grouping of

74

society. Not that there weren't plenty about like us. Single-parent families, I mean, though Gran was a bonus I didn't fully appreciate at the time.

It was Gran who was always there when I came home from school. She often sent me off in the mornings, too, when mum slept in after evening jobs. Mum had a variety of jobs, all as far as I could make out low key, and low paid, despite her obvious intelligence. She worked in kitchens, cleaned offices, helped in bars, worked in shops, that sort of thing. For a time she was even one of the dinner ladies at our primary school, and I was quite proud of this because the dinner ladies were popular.

In the early years, when I was packed off to bed early, Mum and Gran talked and talked, far into the night, and often I would creep out onto the landing and lie holding the banister rails, with my head pressed into a gap, just listening to the voices rising and falling, a comforting sound, the poetry of emotions being voiced with hardly ever a distinct word. After a while I would feel my eyelids drooping and take myself sleepily to my bed. Sometimes, I'm told, I was picked up asleep off the landing, never fully roused, and carried to bed when the two of them finally came upstairs.

Mum arranged things for the three of us (later just Mum and me) to do at weekends, like bus and train trips, walks. She loved walking, especially country walks, woods, hilltops and rivers. Then she and Gran would reminisce about Mum's father, my grandfather who I never knew, and how he loved to fish. We had holidays, too: brief interludes by the sea, mostly at a little place called Seaton, in Cornwall, not far to the west of Plymouth, where we travelled by train first, then a bus. I think we first went to the wooden chalet there after seeing an advert for it on a card in some shop window, possibly Singh's, but perhaps before he bought the shop. We never owned a car. Mum had friends, women and men, but they rarely came to the house. Sometimes they would stop after meeting in the street, chat, while I held on to Mum's hand and waited, tugging with impatience to be off.

Gran was a ferocious smoker. Perhaps the slipstream effect of this was at last affecting Mum. Gran coughed herself away to nothing in just a few weeks all told one hot summer, when I was 12, and they took her off to hospital in the last days and I never saw her again. Then it was just Mum and me. In retrospect they did a great job. I never felt shabby or underprivileged, but there must have been sacrifices behind that. However, despite the low wages, Mum had managed to get a mortgage on our house, a corporation property, when the right to buy came along. Now I know we virtually own it. The pity is she can't have long to enjoy triumphs like this, if I let myself be realistic. Does she know this? I'm sure she does.

***

It is nearly five o'clock when I descend again into the Tap. It is quiet, surprisingly empty, just a handful of people I don't know by the bar, which has benefited greatly from the clean-up though there's still the musty aroma of stale beer and fags. Only a handful of people are there. I'm quite surprised to see one is Ballard, sitting alone in about the same spot he occupied earlier. He is looking at a full pint, elbows on the table, his head between his hands. I buy a bottle of lager and take it over to his table.

"Hi!"

He looks up, gloomy.

"Well, and hi to you too, young Walker," he says, brightening a degree or two. "At last, someone with a bit of stamina. I don't know what the youth of today is coming to, do you? We used to party for days at a time, with all the sex and substance abuse and rock and roll you can imagine. Days!"

"Nobody else here yet?" I say.

"Wimps! Wimps, the lot of them. Excepting present company of course. Siddown."

I do, and as my angle on his face changes I see he is more than a bit the worse for wear. As for the absent others, those who haven't met the 'four, in the door' deadline, I am not entirely surprised. Many must have jobs, others have classes to attend at the college. The whacky four o'clock starting time for the World Cup Wake has been his decision alone. The odd and unaccountable hours of serving the printing presses have put him out of step with the pressing duties of normal folk. I begin to kick myself mentally for not realising the party could be some time starting, but it is too late now to go away.

"Crap game, wasn't it?" he says.

Ah, at last. Just me and him and no interruptions, and as far as I know plenty of time to talk about that game. Maybe coming early to the wake is a good thing after all.

"It had its good points," I start.

"Crap!" he says. "Absolute crap. How's your mum?"

Once again, the memory of the kick-off fades, the ball shooting away on another tangent into dark oblivion.

"Do you know my Mum?"

I remember Mum's silence when I asked her much the same question about Ballard. My curiosity is aroused.

He looks at me closely, as if he is searching my face for something while he curls one of his ringlets around his finger. Perhaps he is trying to assess how carefully he should tread?

"Of course," he says at last. "Everyone knew your mum. She was a real foxy lady. We grew up together. It was the sixties, right?"

He raises one arm, makes a peace-and-love salute.

I have never heard Mum spoken about in the terms Ballard has just used and I find myself suddenly fighting several emotions, especially indignation. But I suppress it because I want to hear what he has to say, especially now that he looks hungover and off guard. 'Foxy' has a special meaning, hasn't it?

But he laughs. I think he sees he has overstepped things, said too much perhaps. He pulls himself up straight. His tone turns to apologetic, or as near to apologetic as I guess Ballard can get.

"God, sorry, I don't mean anything by that ... look, how can I explain? We were young, like you are now. The times were wild. You know how things are. She's a lovely lady your mum. We were partners for a while. Did she tell you that? And I'm really sorry she isn't well, I mean it. That's tough. Perhaps I should go and see her?"

I hardly know what to say, rebuilding the picture of Mum in my mind at the same time thinking how such events might fit with my own life. It crosses my mind again – not a great shock – that there could even be the possibility Ballard is the errant father I long to find out about.

"She ... she mentioned your name," I tell him.

78

He looks disappointed.

"From time to time she talks of you," I add quickly. A lie. My most recent conversation with Mum had been the very first time Ballard's name had cropped up. I am however beginning to see I will have to fit her into the new context that has just been sketched by Ballard, and whether I like it or not, whatever he said would have to be somewhere near the truth.

"We were great travellers, you know. Everywhere. The States, California even, Spain, North Africa, Marrakesh, Israel ... she told you all this?"

I nod, even though this is the first time I have heard of a few lost chapters in Mum's life. The last-named place particularly makes me prick up my ears, because I didn't know she ever went to Israel. I know she has been to the other places. I've seen pictures, although I didn't quite wig that all or any of it had been in the company of Ballard. Somebody always has to hold the camera, right?

But Israel. She never talked about this and there are certainly no pictures recording the excursion, at least none I've seen. And another reason I take special notice of the reference is that Israel is where local rumours about Ballard's murkiest deeds have come from. Perhaps he is confusing her with somebody else?

"Mum? She was in Israel with you?"

"She didn't tell you?"

I shake my head, realising that perhaps everything she has ever told me about the past has been carefully edited.

"Not a word."

Ballard looks down at the table, sombre. "Bad place," he says, shaking his head as if trying to lose unpleasant recollections, "Perhaps she doesn't want to remember all that."

"Bad?"

"Real bad." He has slipped into American beat argot apt for the period he is describing. As he does so he starts sort of falling forward, slumping so that his lolling head is getting closer to the table. Once again, the boozy morning is catching up with him. "Real, real bad. But that's all gone now. It's history. It doesn't matter."

Just for a moment I think he is going to collapse over the table, but he pulls his head up, parts his blonde curls with a flick of his hand and looks straight at me.

"She was a great lady, your Mum."

"Is," I correct him.

"Is, I mean, of course. But there's things best left forgotten."

I can't let him get away with that.

"Forgotten? What – the bad things?"

He nods, looking pained. "Especially one. We agreed we wouldn't ever say anything about it. Ever."

"You'd better tell me."

He knows I can't let it drop.

"It's my Mum, see. And I won't tell anyone."

I am surprised by my new confidence, but then today I have started to find myself at the receiving end of a few surprises already. I am beginning to feel a bit like a target in a fairground range.

Ballard gives me a long, hard look.

"Not even her ... you won't let her know I told you anything?"

Almost a plea. Of course, I agree. I must so that I get the story out of him. But whether or not I will keep the promise ... well, it depends on what he has to say, doesn't it?

A long and awkward silence follows. I can't draw my eyes from his face, but I am aware there are more people coming into the Tap now. For the moment, though, we appear to be in our own small island of solitude, Ballard and me.

"Okay," he says eventually, and I know I have won. "Here's the thing. We've been out there for a while, me and your mum, right, and kibbutz life is really pissing us off, so we decide to take a trip down to Eilat. It's on the Red Sea, and a really long way, right across the Negev. You've heard of the Negev?"

I nod. "The desert."

"Yeah, the desert. The big, dry, empty bloody desert. And we're hitching, of course, because everyone does – did – then. Probably they still do in Israel, it's that sort of place. Anyway, we're on the edge of some Arab town somewhere with just the Negev between us and Eilat, which at that time is like, well, a hippy village, everyone living on the beach, peace, love, bags of dope and all that. And warm sea, too, which will be nice because winter is coming on up in the North. Anyway, there we are hitching when a jeep pulls up. We can see it's an Arab. We had to be careful about Arabs then, just like they do in Israel now. It's always a mess, they're at each other's throats all the time. Anyway, it's been a long time since anything came along so we went with him. He's going all the way he says. I'm worried about Mary...your Mum, I mean. I always worried about her, you

81

know, with the men. But this one seems to be all right and not hassly, except after a while he starts asking us about how much money we are carrying. I try to explain that we are broke because you could only leave England with £50 each at that time – can you believe it, just £50? – but it's hard work.

Eventually, however, he gets the message that we have sod-all money. Even our watches are cheap. And the bastard stops the jeep, there and then, and invites us to get out. In the desert, miles from anywhere. Mary's in tears, pleading, because it's so hot, man. Even riding along in an open jeep it was hot. The wind is like a blowtorch. But he won't listen. All he does is point down the road and say 'Timna. Timna'. It's a place, a copper mine, but I didn't know that at the time. Anyway, it's about 40km down the track and we've just drunk the last of our water and we're somewhere that even Jesus Christ was tempted to sell his soul. Bastard!"

Now I'm intrigued. Was this the point a particularly evil crime attributed to Ballard was committed, I wonder, bringing the legend to mind? Or maybe all that was speculative fancy on the part of malicious gossips, and the predicament of this hapless pair was the 'bad thing' in its entirety. It certainly seems bad enough, stuck without water in the desert.

"Shit," I agree. "What a bastard. So what did you do?"

I mean, they clearly had to do something, or they wouldn't both still be around, would they? Neither would I, come to that.

"There wasn't anything we could do. That's what it looked like. It was a real mess," says Ballard.

At this point he takes a long swig from his relatively untouched pint, as if he is reliving the effect of that fearful, dusty heat. I can now almost feel the glare and hopelessness of it all, and I drain my drink too, set the bottle down, all ears. To my surprise somebody reaches over my shoulder, the empty is lifted from the table and another full one is put in its place. I look up to see my old benefactor, Mick Shoebury, winking.

"Compliments of the house," he says. "Some guy paid for it and never touched it. Go flat if it's left any longer." He drifts away again again, in his shadowy way.

"Jesus!" exclaims Ballard, looking quite glad to break from his narrative. "Bit generous for Shoehorn, isn't it? What have you done to deserve this?"

"Nothing," I say. "It's been a strange sort of day. Really strange." And it had. But it is getting stranger by the minute. And I am starting to tie up a lot of the happenings with one common factor: Mum.

I am anxious for him to continue.

"But you made it, though," I say.

"We watched that bastard go until he vanished, a dot on the horizon. Then we walked for a bit, but it was hopeless. I think Mary was delirious at this stage and I was feeling it was all my fault for getting us into the mess and suggested we laid up for a while if we could find any shade and try to move on again when it was darker and perhaps cooler. They always tell you this is how people manage to survive in the desert, but now the reality of our situation was coming home to us. Desperate.

"The desert road runs along a fairly flat plain and to find any sort of shade we had to break away from it to get to low hills and dry wadis about half a mile away. Even hotter on the sand, it was. By the road at least there was the odd poisonous looking shrub and some big, slow noisy brown grasshoppers but out here there was nothing, not a blade of grass, not a sound. But, glory alleluia, the sun was getting lower and after a while we found a bit of shade in a wadi, and at last there was a slightly lower temperature, but not much. It gets up to 50 degrees, more, and that's in centigrade. We just sort of huddled there in a puddle of shade, hardly daring to move.

"When it was dusk, we started to go back to the road. It was really hard to get moving. All the exposed bits of us, mainly our legs, were coming up in big white blisters, full of water. That's dehydration man. We're leaking water, man, when we haven't a drop to drink. And our feet and ankles were swelling up too, and our bones hurt like they'd been cooked. The next stage is heat stroke, when the body fluids start coming to the surface like that. It's a killer, a real killer. You need litres of water a day to rehydrate, salts too, or you die, and we'd got nothing. And we're running out of luck with any more chances if we go back to the road because now there's no traffic, nothing, because it's Friday, the bloody sabbath, and we know there won't be so much as a bicycle along this God-forsaken road tomorrow either, not until the next sunset when the sabbath ends.

"I would have given up there and then, but I thought we had to keep going as if it was remotely hopeful for Mary's sake. That was when we saw the light. It was well off to the left, back in the wadis, and it was our only hope, so we made our way towards it. There was only starlight but as we got near it was enough to make out a black tent, quite big, and there was a mule, a dog and a goat outside, all tied up to an iron pole driven in the ground. The dog didn't make a sound, just the tip of its tail wagged. Nearer, some light was showing through the thin open weave of the black material and as we got even closer, we could see through. It was just one man, sitting cross-legged on a mat, drinking a cup of tea, with a pile of belongings to one side. He'd have water, obviously, not just to make the tea but because everyone had to have water to live out here and he clearly knew how to survive. He suddenly heard us or sensed us and put the glass down, got up, and came to the tent entrance."

Ballard pauses to empty his glass. I try to picture Mum there, pinching myself because this is all so hard to believe. The pair might look the worse for wear coming out of the desert night, I think, but she'd have that smile, her irresistible smile, I guess, with loads of mascara round those grey-green eyes. Ballard would be in his hippie long hair, probably lots longer than today. It now only reaches his shoulders. Sheepskin jackets wouldn't have done in that climate, although Mum might have carried one, and if their legs were burned that meant shorts. Cut-off jeans? In Mum's case probably too short for modesty in a country where there were many Muslims. Denim shirts, of course.

"He saved you, then? Saved your lives?" I say.

Ballard frowns, and I realise it wasn't quite like that.

"Not really. He invites us in with that gracious sweep of the arm you'd expect, just like a scene from Aladdin or the Arabian Nights. I'll never forget that. We didn't know any Arabic. I think Mary was saying, 'Water, water', while I tried the Hebrew version which I'd picked up, 'Myim, myim,' but he saw at once our predicament, told us to sit and gave us each one of those tiny tea glasses of water from a skin bag, then started to make more tea, boiling a kettle on a little spirit stove. He was a thin, wrinkled man but you never know quite how old they are. He could have been ancient. He had an old voice. Mary put up her glass for more water and he nodded his head, but I think that meant 'no' because he made no move to give her any. I raised my glass too, but he shrugged, picked up his water bag and dangled it in front of our eyes, just to show us how little he had for himself, especially after this unexpected hospitality. There was about a litre, I guess, and I did some quick calculations. 'Shit,' I said to your Mum, hoping he didn't understand English, 'I don't think there's enough to get three of us out of this. It would be touch-and-go for two even'. I think it was then she really expected we would die. So did I, come to that. But I had a bit of an idea. Not a pretty idea. You won't like it. I told Mary to keep his attention while I made a charade of having a pee and excused myself from the tent..."

I listen with horrified fascination, the scene he paints becoming vivid in my mind, like a film. Mum sits before the old man, transfixing him with those beautiful eyes. He is glad, no doubt, to have this vision of paradise before him, alone, if only for the last few moments he has left on earth. She gives nothing away when Ballard creeps back in, the heavy iron pole that had tethered the animals held up in both hands, and she smiles for distraction's sake as he raises it and brings it crashing down on the back of the old man's skull. Once is enough. He just rolls over. They take the water and flee. Throughout, though no longer tethered, the animals keep in their place, noiseless. Ballard and Mum, their master's assassins, vanish into the hot and sandy dark and the dog does not even bark.

"You *murdered* him!"

I am shocked, appalled. The room spins.

"We did, I think."

Ballard's head falls again, this time touching the table, like a supplication.

Those four words, quiet and undramatic, are a stunner. I am shaking all over, my pulse is racing. The 'we' you see makes mum complicit, which of course she was. An accomplice, a murderess. So I am the son of a murderess...

For a moment I do not know what to do. I have an urge to rise and rush out and home and confront her with this, demand to know whether it is true. I also want to grab Ballard, shake him, and make him either repeat or deny what he just said. Instead I do neither. I have not the slightest doubt from the way he says it that it has happened more or less as he recounted it, and nothing anyone can say or do can change that.

"You could have just stolen the water, surely?"

Ballard rouses himself again and shakes his head. He avoids meeting my eyes. "I didn't know how strong he was. We were in a bad way, remember. Besides, if we took his water, he would die anyway."

"He'd have had a chance, at least."

Another shake of the head. "I don't think so. And if he did, he'd be after us, or the police would, for leaving him to die. As it was we felt pretty damn guilty. I can tell you I still feel guilty. It's not something I'm at all proud of."

"Did anyone find him?"

"I don't think so. I don't know. Probably still lying there."

Lying in the sand with the remains of the mule and the dog and the goat. I think of the grim little mummified tableau in the wasteland.

"It was two lives for the price of one," Ballard goes on. "And he was getting on, remember. What would you have done? Think about it. We didn't like what we did, it was the worst thing on earth. But we only survived because of it."

The thought of the faithful animals withering away beside the tent and their dead master brings me near to tears.

"Things were never quite the same with us after that," he says matter-of-factly. "We got within sight of the copper mine, and they saw us coming and sent a truck full of guards to investigate who we were. Workers there had to travel in armed convoys because of militant bandits in the hills around. Turns out it's the original site of King Solomon's mines. Whatever, they were used to people getting heat stroke and they had all the recovery stuff necessary on hand. Eventually, I ended up working at the mine because we needed money to get back home."

He looks at me finally, trying to read me. "I'm sorry," he says, his eyes seeking pity, "This is all a bit of a shock for you, isn't it?"

But I can only shrug, astonished.

"I didn't know anything about it before. Really, she never said anything," I say, but I think I should I be doing something stronger ... calling the police, perhaps?

"Please don't tell her I told you. We vowed we wouldn't tell anyone. I've only let a bit slip, once, and not all the story, but I regretted it. Don't tell anyone, and her especially. Please." There is now real agony in his face. "If anyone says anything to her it should be me. I should go and see her. Yes, I should. I will."

"It might be a good idea," I say, "But tell me, you're saying she actually helped you kill someone, in cold blood?"

"Don't look so shocked. Worse things have happened."

"Not often."

"No, I suppose not. But you won't say anything?"

"I won't," I say, uncertain if I can keep my word on such an astonishing issue. "It is true though, isn't it? I can tell."

He nods. It was a long ago, he says. Time and distance made it unreal. And there was another fact to think of too, one that has already crossed my mind: if this hadn't happened, I probably would not be here.

He finishes by appealing once again.

"Really, you won't say anything?"

"I won't."

His shoulders lift.

"Good. Thanks. Not that anybody would believe it all, not now, after all this time. I'd just deny it. No way of proving it."

Possibly he is right.

"Tell me," I say, another issue finding its way into my consciousness to join the startling images of Ballard's recent revelations, "When did you and Mum break up? Why?"

It was late 1969 or 70 he says, but in reality, they had stopped being an item ever since the desert incident.

"You know, it was the year someone first walked on the moon," he says.

I didn't know, but it rules Ballard out as the answer to one of my problems.

"You don't know who she went out with after?"

He thinks. After a while, he says: "There was a whole bunch of admirers – Roger Stenton, John Cannock, even old Shoeface, Ginger Selincourt, Ryan Makim. And then there was Derek the aimless drifter of course ... no, I don't know for sure if she hitched up with anyone in particular. Why?"

I can see he knows why I am asking the moment he finishes. But I have no chance to put it into words even if I want to be so transparent (which I don't), because the large girl I had been sitting next to in the Tap earlier in the day suddenly appears behind Ballard. She claps her hands over his eyes and pulls his head back to engulf it in her ample bosom.

"Guess who?" she says, giving me a conspiratorial wink. I cringe.

"Thunderthighs!" says a mightily relieved Ballard, clearly delighted at the sudden distraction.

"Well?" booms Thunderthighs, as if she has been predestined to appear at this very moment to extricate him from a difficult situation. "Are we going to party, or what?"

Chapter 7 Follow the yellow p***k Toad

How would you feel if you just learned your mother was a killer, and a cold-blooded killer at that? It amounts to that, doesn't it, even if she was doing it to save her own life?

But I can't quite accept the fact, while knowing beyond doubt that it is true, that Ballard is not lying. Why should he? I just don't want to think of her like that.

Not only was there the killing, but Mum is now revealed as someone who really, seriously knocked around a bit in the old relationship game. But perhaps it's just like people say it is and everyone was loose with their associations in those peace-and-love days.

What I want to do at this moment is crawl away from it all, go home, adjust, take it all in, talk to the Mum I thought I knew, not someone I clearly don't know well at all. She'll have to respond, won't she? Sick or well, she'll have to tell me about all that.

I try again to cast Ballard as a journalist used to embroidering his tale, but once again I see this is too elaborate to be nonsense, even for somebody in a notoriously unreliable profession.

I realise I *should* go home of course, creeping away while Ballard engages Thunderthighs in meaningless wordy banter. But I am rooted here. I also feel I've lost something. Was Mum somehow part of my self-image? I can't put my finger on it, but just a few words from a less than sober man have knocked the stuffing out of me. They've also taken my legs away.

While I dither others start to arrive, filling in spaces around the table. I look on, detached, in a bemused state, as the whole party thing starts to rev up again. Somewhere outside of the dumbfounded creature I have become, I realise, there is excitement in the air, like electricity. And then another full bottle of lager is lowered in front of me.

"There you go kid. Cheer up!"

It's that pseudo-beat drawl again. I look up to see Ballard is no longer sitting where he was. Now he is standing directly behind me and has bought me a drink. I hadn't noticed him go to the bar or come back. And we have somehow become best mates in our recent exchange, it seems. Or perhaps I should say fellow conspirators. I pick up the bottle and drink.

I'm still out of it, however. For long lost moments I feel a bit like the missing part of a cogwheel, everything else racing along and leaving me out of gear, disengaged. But after a while the drink starts to fix that for me after a bit. It might be helping because I have already had heaps of alcohol that day. Might even be something Ballard has put in the drink. Who knows? However, one minute I am out of everything, the next minute I am back, released from introspection.

I take it in that the party crowd is now gathering around two big tables, one of which I am sitting at, in roughly the same area as earlier that day. Some of the two conjoined groups are sitting, some standing, and many are carrying bottles or off-licence plastic bags, or have set bags and bottles on the tables in front of them. The promised 'lark in the park' is obviously still on. One boy I recognise even carries an enormous boom-box portable radio, perched (silent for the moment) on his shoulder. Somebody not far from him has lined up a row of Es on the tabletop. Money is crossing the table as he deals out pill after pill off the end of the line. The joint-rollers are busy once again, too.

I take another pull at the bottle, and I am suddenly aware of a rowdy exchange as the additional dose kicks in ever more solidly.

"And tell us, fair TITania, who your boyfriend is to be this fine night?"

Ballard, still standing behind me, directs his voice to Thunderthighs, who is now seated opposite, and puts heavy emphasis on the 'Tit' bit of 'Titania'.

At this Thunderthighs feigns coyness and assumes a bumpkin accent – neither of these making for an altogether a pretty effect, but sort of funny, or at least that is the way it seems to me and a few others who are probably just as pissed as I am.

"Why, sir, 'tis 'im, Oberon."

I laugh with the others, but it is still the laugh of one who has not yet fully realised the full extent of what's in play.

"*Oberon*?" says Ballard. "Ah, you mean 'im Oberon the other table, yes? Don't tell us, it's Toad, isn't it?"

More laughter. Murderer or not, Ballard does have a way with words. And Throgmore, alias Toad, is indeed sitting at the other table, a so-far quite good-natured Throgmore. He stands up. "Ugh!" he exclaims, "Not my sort of ass I fear. I think you should be the one to get to the *Bottom* of it."

"Touché!" rejoins Ballard and, clearly not wishing to be knocked off his pedestal as the town's acknowledged chief word-tosser, he adds: "But hey, who gives a Puck!"

Of course, they're Midsummer Night's Dream characters! The booze-soaked loose marbles in my head momentarily roll together and form a semi-coherent chain. And it is Midsummer

Night, of course! Today, the day of the ill-fated match. Tonight rather, this evening, now!

The new wave of laughter subsides, and I can see Throgmore's brow furling with the effort of finding something to say back quick. But he can't dredge anything up. He isn't really fast-witted enough, at least not with this game, and in the end, you can see he realises too much time has elapsed for a rejoinder. He sits down, embarrassed. Signs of truculence begin to appear – a tic in the cheek, a deepening glower. These giveaways are a red rag to Ballard of course...

"Not like Mr Toad to be lost for words. Parp Parp!"

Ballard's grip tightens on the back of my chair I can feel. He is steeling himself in case this battle gets out of hand. He's possibly not all that sure that he can handle an enraged Toad, who is younger than him by half, after all.

"Leave it, ball-breaker!"

The unexpected, growled caution comes from next to me, and for the first time I notice Becky Jackson is sitting there. In a calm but strong voice she looks up and adds: "You're a real shit Ballard, don't stir it. Leave him."

She looks at me.

"He's a shit, isn't he?"

Uncharacteristically perhaps, Ballard does take her advice and lays off. He looks away from Throgmore, and the tension subsides.

At this point Becky nudges me just as I'm slipping off into a self-absorbed trance again.

"I don't know why they look up to him, do you? Bloody fools. Ballard's only a superannuated hack, and they think he's some bloody guru or something."

This is embarrassing, because Ballard is still holding the back of my chair and I know he can hear every word she is saying, even if others can't. His grip on the chair becomes tense again. But surprisingly, rather than rising to a new challenge, he pretends he didn't hear. He lets go of my chair, moves away.

"There, that's better, isn't it?" says my new companion. It's probably the longest conversation I had ever had with Becky, except that I haven't yet contributed anything myself.

"Cool," I say, and suddenly finding something else apt springing up unbidden from the memory banks at the back of my head, "Blessed are the peacemakers."

Becky seems to like that and moves closer.

What is going on? In the space of not much more than a couple of hours I have apparently become much more acceptable to the opposite sex, more so than at any other time in my life. And and here with Becky is yet another chance, I realise, to break my duck, make a move. But still, something holds me back. It may be I can't quite see Becky in these terms. In fact, she rather frightens me, always has. Perhaps she frightens Ballard too? It isn't the spectacles, even though they do make her eyes very big and intense. It is ... well, something I can't define. Perhaps it is because she is super-bright, always top of the form.

At this moment I desperately want to see if Glynnis has turned up, or even Carol Latham, and I look round the tables.

95

Not there, either of them. But my pal Roy is, although I see he now has a crepe bandage sling in addition to the plastered leg he had first thing this morning. He has appeared behind Thunderthighs. What looks suspiciously like a fresh plaster is visible beneath the sling. He hasn't broken something else, has he? It is the opposite arm to the leg, and I see he is now supported with a crutch. That's new. At least today it is. "Drink?" he croaks at me, briefly letting go of the crutch rung to mime sipping.

"Jesus," says Becky in my ear, aghast, "What's the poor bastard done now?"

I tap my own arm in the area that corresponds to Roy's new injury and give him a quizzical look. He looks down at the bandaged limb and back at me as if surprised it is still there, and certainly surprised anybody should think it is worthy of any attention.

"Broken," he shouts matter-of-factly over the hubbub, breaking into a broad grin. "Fell downstairs this afternoon. Do you want a drink or don't you?"

"Not now."

I shake my head. He shrugs as well as he is able, clutches his crutch again, turns and hobbles off to the now quite crowded bar. I lean back to find Becky is still pressing quite close to me and a question bubbles up.

"Becky, your dad, when he was younger, like us now, did he ... does he ever say anything about it? What girlfriends he had, things like that?"

Becky always gave things serious thought. However I do not have long to wait for a reply.

"No. Why?"

"No matter."

I look away, hoping the pub's gathering smoky gloom is covering my growing blush. It does matter of course, it always will, especially now, after that conversation with Ballard.

By the time I turn back Becky has started talking to someone I don't recognise on her other side, and I once again fall into a bubble of solitude. But not for long. Ballard, who has now moved round the table again and squeezed himself in beside Thunderthighs, raps on the table with an empty bottle.

"Well, you bunch of fairies, or whatever you are, shall we go to the park?"

There is general murmuring and shuffling of feet, and some stand up as if ready to move. But they are stopped short by a voice of dissent, clear above the hum.

"Don't be daft. They'll be on to us. Leave it till later."

Throgmore again. But now Toad is flushed and resurgently confident with drink. I can see Ballard start to bristle. He sneers.

"Shit, Toad. I told you, there's only one copper in town and he's scared out of his wits. There's nothing to stop us. Nothing."

But Throgmore will not be done down.

"Don't listen to him," he urges the wavering crowd. "He's probably cooked the whole wake thing up to get a story for his bloody paper. He's bloody daft enough. Fuckin' mad."

"You're mad. He's the mad one!" retorts Ballard.

"Not! It's you!"

Both are on their feet now, aware they are starting to slide into a childish slanging match. But they seem powerless to stop it. The other partygoers are now frozen on the spot, some in the act of rising, some already standing and ready to go.

"No, Toad, it's you. You're a p***k. Ladies and gentlemen, fellow fairies and sprites, Toad is a p***k."

At this Throgmore lurches towards Ballard but he has a long way to go. People near him step forward and try to grab at him to nip the thing in the bud. Others, however, mutter encouragement, clearly excited by the prospect of a fight.

"I'm not," Toad growls, his voice thickening with uncontrollable anger.

Seeing Throgmore is about to be safely restrained, Ballard goes a step further. "What's more, you're a yellow p***k!" he taunts as the would-be assailant is gripped by both arms.

"Not!"

"Oh yes you are!"

"Not!"

"Prove it..."

Throgmore looks wildly around the room, but this only serves to make him more aware he's been caught out indulging in a childish rant. However, he finds new resolve from somewhere. Brow knotted with determination he shakes off the restraints, gathers himself. But unfortunately, or fortunately depending on how you look at it, the path to Ballard has been blocked.

"All right then. I'll show you who's yellow – I'm off to the park for a real party. Come on!" Throgmore's red face glares once more around the audience. And then he turns on his heel and makes for the steps.

There is a collective gasp and a gap of milliseconds while people ponder what to do, but the ever-resourceful Ballard is quick to leap at the new opening that has fallen into his lap.

"Come on, what are you all waiting for?" he shouts, springing to follow on the heels of the tormented Throgmore. It is as if he has entirely engineered a perfect act of showmanship, even down to being provided with just the right words, words which make him smile with mischievous glee:

"Follow Toad. Follow the yellow p***k Toad!"

Some are slow to catch on, others quicker, forming a chain behind Ballard and joining in the infectious chant as he heads across the bar to the stairway, and on, up and up, the chant growing, swelling.

*"Follow the yellow p***k Toad, follow the yellow p***k Toad, follow, follow, follow, follow, follow the yellow p***k Toad..."*

Mouths fall open. An astonished silence comes over the rest of the tipplers in the pub as an unlikely and quickly growing conga dance forms and winds its way through them and up and out towards the open air, swaying crazily and roaring with increasing volume.

*"... follow the yellow p***k Toad, follow the yellow p***k Toad..."*

I find it infectious, impossible not to join in, and I insert myself not all that far from the front of the action. As I do so I'm grabbed from behind as the snake grows.

*"...follow the yellow p***k Toad, follow the yellow p***k Toad, follow, follow, follow, follow, follow the yellow p***k Toad..."*

Quite soon it is a very long conga. As we emerge from the Tap, I have a brief glimpse of the lone figure of Throgmore stomping along and no doubt still fuming way out ahead, but now not all that far behind him at the front of our chain is Ballard, always ready to milk a situation, following Throgmore's course into the Town Square. The town's one on-duty policeman has moved aside into the shadows of the shopping arcade. The officer is talking desperately into his mobile while the conga executes a double lap of honour round the Square, the serpent's tail lashing wildly in high spirits accompanied by the clash of glass bottles, the duller rattle of cans and the undiminished chant.:

"...*follow the yellow p***k Toad, follow, follow, follow, follow, follow the yellow p***k Toad...*"

As we peel off the Square Ballard follows Throgmore, who is now heading for the park. Dusk is gathering.

"... *follow the yellow p***k Toad, follow the yellow p***k Toad, follow, follow, follow, follow, follow the yellow p***k Toad...*"

I don't know what makes me look back, but I see that far beyond the end of the writhing conga tail there is a lone struggling figure following on crutches. Roy of course. And an image flashes through my mind of the little cripple boy trying to catch up with the Pied Piper of Hamelin...

I realise we must by now be quite a sight, this fantastic many-legged drunken animal. There is very little traffic but what vehicles there are slow almost to a stop as the crazy creature passes, and so do astonished walkers. A bloke on a bike nearly falls off, wobbling like a circus clown.

And then somewhere between the Tap and the park main entrance our beat changes to a resounding rumba, still interspersed with occasional snatches of '*The Yellow P***k Toad*'. We snake into the open pedestrian gateway at the side of the big, locked iron gates, weaving between monstrous plane trees as we start down a darkening avenue of chestnuts, some of their upper branches still aglow with late blossom, like Christmas candles. Now voices are even less restrained.

The whole effect is fantastic. I have never seen anything like this before. It feels so ... well, anarchic, liberating. Is this what it might be like breaking away, changing my life as Mum had suggested, leaving town ... just as she and Ballard had done? It feels suddenly as if I have shrugged off something that has been bogging me down for years, like casting off a heavy winter coat that is now too hot. The the next link in the chain ahead of me, a bloke I only vaguely know, looks back every now and then, a huge grin all over his face, and I can see I am not the only one enjoying this experience. And when I turn to look at the woman behind, again somebody I don't know, it is the same. I can't remember feeling so good and I'm sure I show it too.

"*Da da da da boom boom! Da da da da boom boom! Da da da da ...*" we now chant.

We plunge into the grove of cherry trees outside the park's public conveniences, roaring with laughter as we skirt a sudden grotesque lamplit tableau of two standing men, trousers dropped and faces foolish with discovery, caught astonished in a frozen act of gay sex. Other mackintoshed figures with presumably similar pursuits stare with surprise then melt into the gloomy shrubbery.

"...boom boom! Da da da da boom boom! Da da da da boom boom! ..."

On we go, on and on, round the playground swings, past the foot of the slide and round a knot of solemn heavy-lidded ten-year-olds looking up from huddling over a tin of glue while one of them falls backwards noiselessly into a litter of messy plastic bags.

"... Da da da da boom boom! Da da da da boom boom!..."

We pass a firelit semi-circle of the town's derelicts, pausing with plastic cider-bottles raised to their flushed and mostly familiar faces...

"....boom boom!..."

And finally, as we snake out into the wide-open grassy slope leading down towards the boating lake, the chant dies, and a wild, whooping rush heads for the waterside.

Under more chestnuts there is a fireside gathering of ten or a dozen people perhaps, many children too and as we rush towards them, they shrink back to hover in the shadows. The adults clearly don't want to be recognised, but the children surge forward.

The man who was just ahead of me in the conga hisses: "It's the Albanians. Hold onto your wallet!" but before we know it the horde of kids is among us, running beside us with outstretched hands, palms up, eyes pleading.

My informant is no doubt correct about their origins: there is a lorry depot at the side of the park and the rumour is that some drivers are coining it with very lucrative cargos of illegal immigrants. A little dark girl, very slight, latches onto me and will not go. If I look away, she runs to put herself wherever I am looking. But we are both of us swept along by the tide and I have to concentrate on not losing my footing.

By the time I arrive, breathless, at the bottom, I think I have given my new little companion the slip. She has either been left behind or has vanished to pester somebody else. But it is not so. She appears again seconds later, face full of pleading, her little hand again outstretched.

"No!" I say, sternly this time, holding up my palms. "I have no money."

Her eyes drop. For a moment she stands as if absorbing this, but then to my relief she turns and disappears into the darkness. But relief is swiftly followed by remorse. I am on the dole and the money doesn't last all that long, this week's dosh already vanishing quicker than most, some on the half bottle of Scotch in my pocket which I bought on my way to my second visit to the Tap that day. But I do have some loose change in my pocket which I could have given her without any great loss. After all, when it is gone, it is gone. I feel sorry, knowing she has to be far from as lucky as I am. When I think of it, the men, women and other children she is with are all probably on the verge of starvation.

I put it out of mind as I near the lakeside. A small group has already started the party ahead of the Tap mob. Indeed, it appears some must have been there for some time because there is a growing bonfire of fallen branches and some park furniture. There's music too, and I can even hear people splashing about rowdily in the water, accompanied by alarmed calls from the lake's water birds.

As I make my way towards the light one of the fireside figures stands and turns my way, a long coat opens at the front to reveal, like a gash, a red dress. She smiles. Glynnis!

"Good. You came," she says. Warm fingers close round my hand and everything else goes out of focus.

***

Now wasn't this all I had been hoping for. Of course it was. I wished this very situation would come to pass, that she and I would meet and all the frustration and fears about my sexuality would be swept aside, that we would become ... well, perhaps not lovers just yet, for a start at any rate, although there was the best chance ever this might be the night ...

"Come on. Over here."

She tugs at my hand.

I would have gone anywhere with her, but we do not go far from the fireside and the rest of the party, just far enough into the gloom to be out of earshot and recognition.

"Look," she says, suddenly earnest, "I'm splitting. Do you want to come with me?"

She is slightly shorter than me without her high heels. Her face turns up to mine, catching a flicker from the fire as a log flares up.

"What, *now*?"

A puzzled look crosses her face, then a dawn of comprehension. She becomes even more serious.

"No, not just now. That's not what I meant. I mean I'm going, leaving town. I can't stand any of it any longer. I've quit my job and I'm quitting my flat. I want to go to London, Peter Next

Friday maybe. I just wanted to catch you and ask if you wanted to come too. You don't like this dump any more than me, do you?"

It is an ultimatum I am not prepared for. She is so close, but her unanswered question is like an invisible screen between us as we stand here face to face, hand in hand.

"I don't..." I stumble, desperately wondering what to say. She is beautiful, I realise. All I want is for us to stay like this, here, but I know it can't be. She looks down.

"Sorry," she says. "It's not the time to ask you this, is it? But I felt I had to come and ask. I felt you thought the same way. Perhaps you do. If you must think about it that's all right. But let me know soon. Now I must go."

Another shock.

"You're going now? Leaving the party?"

She lets go of my hand.

"Yes. I must. I told Dad I would go and see them. And I still feel like shit after this morning. I need to sleep it off. But stay and enjoy yourself, eh. And think about going to London."

She stands on tiptoe and kisses me lightly on the cheek. Then she turns and she's gone, moving quickly and silently into the darkness.

I know I want to stop her, but I cannot move. I just stand there, swept by an acute sense of loss.

"Mister, pliss?"

I look down. My little shadow is back, her sad dark eyes widening. She reaches out.

I am about to deny her again but this time she holds her hand out with her fist closed about something, as if she is offering me a gift.

"You take, pliss?"

I put out my hand. She smiles and reaches up to hold on with one hand while she places something in my palm with the other. Then she closes my fingers over it, squeezes tightly.

She steps back, looks up into my face and giggles, then turns and to my relief vanishes into the night.

With my hand still closed around this strange, warm and somewhat sticky nocturnal gift – a happening which helps in some way towards breaking the spell of my frustrated encounter with Glynnis – I turn slowly back towards the fireside, wondering not only about what to do about the proposition that has just been put to me but what to do next, what to do now...

It is only when I feel the warmth of the fire that I find I cannot open my hand. I have been superglued. The gift is probably a small coin from the way it feels: my reward for being a tightwad.

And at that moment an unearthly scream rips out of the darkness beyond the firelight. Everything goes into freeze-frame.

Chapter 8 Firefight

It isn't really extra-dark yet, but when you stare into something bright like a fire then look quickly away, any degree of darkness is almost impenetrable. At the chilling sound of the scream everyone has stopped whatever they are doing. All eyes look towards the noise. Deathly silence follows, broken only by the mad quacking of a startled duck.

I hold my breath. Then a little way off I hear muffled voices, raised. One of them I think might be Glynnis, the other for a moment unidentifiable. This is followed by loud sobbing, slowly retreating.

Everyone is still peering out into the night when a figure, at first indistinct, comes towards us out of the dark. Carol Latham steps into the mothy pool of light cast by the bonfire, an open overcoat over the skimpy outfit I have already seen her in twice today.

She grins and steps to my side. Her hair is all over the place, escaping its carefully made curls, and she has a scratch on her cheek. She also has a sort of flushed, wild look about her, but quickly composes herself.

"Bumped into something," she says, looking incredibly pleased.

People relax, the party resumes. Sticking my glued hand deep in my pocket to avoid having to give explanations for it, I smile.

"I'm glad you're alone now, Pete," she says, moving close.

I hold my breath again. She sort of leans into me. It is my good arm side, fortunately, for almost without thought I raise it to circle her shoulder. It's so natural I hardly know I am doing it. A feeling of oneness envelopes us and we stand in silence, just looking at the noisy crowd in the firelight, the knot of determined dancers and the backdrop of the many like us, me and Carol, who are just standing and watching.

Slowly, her head leans teven nearer to mine and our cheeks touch. Hers is warm and soft, downy as I noticed earlier. And I catch the scent of violet cachous on her breath. I turn face to face with her, and before I know it, we are kissing, my glued hand rising to complete the embrace. Real kissing.

Andrea Twaite never kissed like that. Carol's tongue is long and hot and greedy and when it retreats it draws mine after it. Unlike my few embraces with Angela, there is no doubt at all Carol has breasts, as well as something urgent and insistent going on lower down, thrusting against my thigh.

She draws back once, looking at my face, then grins at the effect she has produced, and we engage again. My disabled hand is all but forgotten.

She moves her mouth to my ear at the next break, whispers: "Come on, let's go."

And she reaches for my hand, luckily my good one, and tugs. We break from the firelit circle and head into the velvet darkness.

***

In my state any woman could have led me as Carol is doing now, you understand. Anyone. Soon we are deep in shrubs and the hubbub and the glow of the fire subsides. Out here the only chance of being discovered will be through couples like us stumbling about in the darkness. She tugs me to a grassy bank screened by large dark plants, rhododendrons I would guess. Then we sit, her first. The grass seems dry. For a moment we simply stay there, still, side by side.

"I brought this, for us."

She pulls a half-bottle from her coat pocket. Unscrewing it she takes a swig and passes it over. Vodka.

The fierce cheap spirit scorches my throat.

"Thanks," I gasp.

Then without warning she is suddenly all over me again, with renewed intensity. My jacket and her coat we wrestle off as best we are able. In a flurry I reach out to find a smooth round curved belly. Her belt is in the way, a barrier. I start to push my fingertips under...

"Sod it!"

Her shout arrests everything and to my dismay she rolls away. She sits up, looks down at her chest with disgust.

"What?" I am bewildered.

"Nothing."

She folds her arms across her still-covered breasts, frowning.

"What?" I say again, leaning closer. I reach to pull at her arm, wanting to see. She lets it fall away without resisting, stares glumly ahead. A large wet patch glistens on her top, a spreading round patch over the area covering her left nipple. That it is breast milk does not register with me immediately.

"Sorry," she says in a small voice. "That keeps happening. Must be feeding time."

She glumly puts her coat back on and does it up, covering her leaking mammary area, while I put on my own jacket, not quite knowing what to do next. I mean, I am in an excited state, but it seems things are over, for the moment at least. I begin to see what it feels like to be one of those creatures that fall in love with impossible unresponsive objects, like hedgehogs mounting a lavatory brush or frogs trying to mate with goldfish.

She puts her hand on my arm.

"It won't always be like this, honest it won't. I promise," she says.

We sit and finish the vodka in silence, my ardour slowly subsiding. I wonder if it is the same anti-climax for her. I guess it must be.

Then a question comes to mind, sneaking through in spite of the circumstances and presenting itself as an imperative.

"Carol, your dad – does he ever say anything about the girls he used to know? Before he met your mum, I mean?"

"Dad? 'E met our mum when they were at school. Childhood sweethearts, like. They got married when they was 18. 'Ad to, I think, cos of me." A giggle. A least she is recovering from our recent setback. No real lead there, however, on my mum's secret past. I feel disappointed yet relieved in a way that her dad was spoken for, but I continue to probe.

"Oh. No sort of monkey-business, like?"

"There was some trouble, I think. Mum says it wasn't all plain sailing."

"Your dad, you mean? He two-timed her? Played around?" It feels grown up to be using these terms.

"It was all right though. She soon put an end to it. Fixed it."

"Fixed it? What do you mean? How?"

"There's ways and means," she says mysteriously, then clams up. She looks away and for moments we sit in silence, apart but together, listening to the *too-wit* of an owl and shouts of distant revelry. So far, my questions have been taking me nowhere. And everywhere. I begin to try again, start defining exactly what I am after...

"And ... do you know if...?" I start, but it is as far as I get.

"Let's go back to the others," she suggests. She's tired of the subject, I can see.

As we walk back towards the glow of the fire she tucks her arm in mine, squeezes.

"It will be all right in a while, that milk thing. It doesn't matter, does it?" she says. "I mean, to ... us?"

At this moment I feel entirely chivalrous towards Carol. Glynnis has vanished from my mind. I give her arm a squeeze back.

"No. It doesn't matter."

Not much it didn't.

She stops suddenly and kisses me on the cheek.

"Good. We going out then?"

I squeeze her arm in reply and we continue through the shrubbery towards the party.

The fire has now been replenished with large branches and what looks like deck chairs. It is wilder and hotter, and clouds of sparks are hurling themselves into the night sky. A big circle has formed about the blaze and faces shine in its light. As we try to slip in unnoticed the ever-irrepressible Ballard is leading the singing of a bawdy rugby song, *If I Were the Marrying Kind*. Some of the blokes in the party look by now well loaded, and even the girls are joining in with enthusiasm. Some of them, anyway. Throgmore, I notice, has passed out completely, and is lying flat on his back. Amazingly, he now seems to be the object of Thunderthighs' attentions. At least she is sitting close to him and has hold of his hand.

Then, alarmingly, Ballard's eye alights on me and Carol just as the last lines of the ditty are closing...

"She'd push hard, I'd push hard, we'd both push hard together, we'd be all right in the middle of the night, pushing hard together..."

Ballard finishes with a theatrical flourish, and with his usual wicked sense of timing gestures our way, projecting his voice while I wish I could be anywhere else ...

"Which no doubt our young friends here can tell us all about eh? What have you been up to in the bushes, we wonder?"

A ragged cheer mocks us. I am mortified. I think Carol must feel the same way but instead she looks pleased with herself. A public confirmation of our oneness, perhaps, like an engagement.

Ballard won't let go.

"Young Walker again. He's a lad, eh? What's this, another woman? How many's that you've had tonight? What happened to the other one?"

I feel Carol's grip tighten. Her mouth comes close to my ear again. "Don't let him get to you," she whispers and then, to my surprise, she raises her voice in response, and it's not without vehemence.

"Just you lay off. She's 'istry, she is. It's none of your business."

A wild "woo-oooooo" breaks from the crowd at this, but for the second time that night I see Ballard hold back, looking down at his feet. When they see there is to be no further contest people start to look away. A vague uneasiness creeps into my mind about what has made Glynnis 'history' and for a moment I remember that earlier awful scream. But there is too much going on to dwell on this.

"Come on, take me home Pete," Carol whispers in my ear. "You can come back here if you like but walk with me through the park. I should go home, see to Toby."

As we set off Ballard is launching into *The Mayor of Bayswater* and the crowd is picking up the tune with him.

The rest of the park seems eerily empty compared with its odd communities of the earlier hours, but we walk briskly as we can through the darker regions. We pause in the pool of light under a street lamp by the main gate. We kiss again, this time with more tenderness and less passion.

"You don't need to come all the way back. I'll see you tomorrow?"

I agree.

"Just don't get off with anyone else, eh?"

"All right. Of course, I mean."

This makes her smile, but then she says with a more serious tone: "She doesn't really mean anything to you, that Glynnis Cannock, does she?"

I shake my head, although I really haven't a clue what Glynnis means or might mean to me.

"N...no."

"Good," she says, disengaging and turning quickly. "Cos I fixed her."

She patters away quickly down the street in her low heels under the new leaves of the lime trees between the park railings on one side and a long row of large dark vans drawn up at the roadside.

She has gone some way before I realise the full significance of her last remark, and what really lay behind the scream in the dark. Another example of the terrible revenge of the Latham women and their power to fix things.

I should have called her back, asked her what degree of physical damage she had wrought on Glynnis, but I let her go, sorting through my thoughts while the silence of the night closes back around me, save for the distant shouts of the wake by the lake.

Out beyond it all the town has by now become a pool of dark silence. It owes me a dad, this town. It owes me a role model, somebody who would help my twisted pangs of anguish, guide me through the snares of these newly pressing relationships.

I start to think maybe I should go home too, back to Mum. Back to make sure she has taken all her pills and is tucked in warmly for the night, although it is not actually cold even this late. Maybe I should also get it all off my chest, get her to tell who my father was, is, hear from her own mouth the truth about the old Arab in the desert. She is the only one who really knows.

I look in the direction of the party. As well as hearing the distant noise I can see where it is from a glow in the sky. The sudden thought comes to me that it is nothing at all to do with football any more, all this, not the World Cup, not anything more than an excuse for ... what, a bit of anarchy? Letting off high spirits? A late attack of spring fever?

Come to think of it, the World Cup failure has not crossed my mind now for some time, although it did start out as the most important thing of the day, the glorious run up to the final challenge, the ignominious yet somehow applaudable ending, Beckham's demise, England's defeat.

A clock chimes. It is the Town Hall in its tinny imitation of Big Ben. Other chimes join in, raggedly out of synch. Eleven o'clock. I shake my head to clear my thoughts, take a deep breath of the cool night air.

I am almost ready to start home, but not far ahead the door of one of the parked vans starts to open, quietly, then another one, and black figures start moving stealthily round to the rear doors which are also being opened. Soon, to my utter amazement, a whole army of policemen in full riot gear is mustering menacingly on the pavement just a few yards away.

Chapter 9 The Riot Act

I guess just what is about to happen. The cops gathering around the paddy wagons can't see me because I'm standing in the shadow of the gate pillar. I know I should make myself scarce and head home, away from certain trouble – it would be easy if I was quick, and wise too – but instead I slip back into the park and start to run, heading blindly into the dark towards the distant glow and noise of the party. I feel I must warn everyone. It just seems the right thing to do.

Once I know I am out of sight of the gathering stormtroopers my feet fairly fly and I give no thought for my safety, careering through shrubs, flowerbeds, goodness knows what. Then suddenly, I am running on air. I have shot into empty space, and I know I must be at the slope down to the lake. I can't see the ground properly. With a jarring thump I touch down and fall winded on the turf. There's also a sharp pain in my left ankle. But knowing what is behind me I scramble back to my feet and run on.

Nearer, I can see the fire is huge now, and as well the party is shifting into a noisier phase. But I reckon I am close enough for them to hear me and I start yelling as I run in.

"Quick! Cops! The cops are coming! Quick, run!"

Not everyone hears me. Ballard does however. He stands up, swaying above the others, scorn on his face.

"Don't be daft! You're kidding, Don't listen to Walker! He's bullshitting!"

But my warning is already too late. There are other entrances to the park and unknown to me there have been more swarms of police gathered all around and closing in. Even before I finish shouting dark figures start to detach themselves from the encircling shrubbery, Perspex shields glinting as they reflect the shooting flames of the bonfire. Mouths fall open in disbelief as the wall of policemen advances, batons held high. Then, at a barked signal, the officers in the lead start to beat a steady and aggressive tattoo on their shields. The drumming is taken up by the others, who are coming on at a steady pace. The distant wail of a siren is growing louder, drawing closer. We are all trapped.

The party spirit dies rapidly, apart from the bass techno beat from a disc player adding a bizarre undertone. There are policemen on all three sides. The only escape route is the lake, and by now the water must surely be too cold for anyone to be daft enough to take that option, I reckon.

But the shield-beaters keep coming on even though they can see we're trapped. Then, at around twenty paces away there is another command, and they all stop, menacing statues, their batons held above their heads. My heart is beating fast, I can hear it pounding. The other partygoers, some now standing, others still sitting or lying, frozen, must feel the same.

In a bizarre twist to this already unbelievable sight an official-looking figure in full dress high-ranking uniform pushes his way through the front line, steps into the clear a couple of paces, and then holds up a sheet of paper in front of his face with both hands. It's a dramatic gesture, like the town crier making a royal proclamation.

"God!" says Ballard in a voice loaded with incredulity, "He's going to read the Riot Act ... he's actually going to read the bloody Riot Act! This is fantastic!"

There's no messing with the words. They ring out, archaic and awful, a dreadful medieval incantation.

But then everyone turns their eyes away because there is a counter attraction.

Beyond the serried ranks of coppers and the Riot Act reader, the headlights of a large vehicle are starting to lurch through the park towards us down the slope, gathering pace. A siren wails again, deafening now, drowning the final words of the statement. A fire truck. The vehicle approaches, slews round broadside to the fire and stops, its headlights glaring out across the lake surface where a spectral mist is starting to rise. Everyone gapes at this new intrusion, including the policemen. Silhouetted figures in helmets are busy on top of the machine. Then there's another command: the police ranks break and fall back a little, only to reform on either side of the truck. And suddenly, without a warning, a jet of water shoots directly into the heart of the fire.

Not a good idea.

A violent explosion of steam and ashes erupts, sending partygoers and policemen alike staggering back enveloped in a choking gas cloud which stings my eyes. And apart from the misty lake surface floodlit by the fire engine's lights, everything is plunged into darkness.

"Run!" Ballard's voice rings out above the confused scene. I am already doing just that.

Partygoers, policemen, firemen – it is hard to tell one from the other – are blundering everywhere in the confusion. There is frenzied shouting, some loud screams. Several people have jumped in the lake, judging by the splashing.

I just keep running despite my bad ankle. Feeling the ground rising under my feet I carry on up the slope, vaguely knowing I will soon find shrubbery to hide in so long as I can outpace any policemen headed this way. I'm actually not a bad runner. At school cross-country had been my speciality. Despite a lack of exercise since then, and despite the recent winding, my breath holds out quite well.

My eyes start to adjust to the gloom, and I can see at last there are some substantial bushes not far ahead. I feel good about that. Maybe there is a chance of getting away now.

But it is not to be, not yet anyway. There is a sudden sharp shout to one side, followed by the yap of an animal, and something winds itself round one of my legs. And I go down with a thump again, just managing to get my hands in place to break my fall. A body rolls against me and a smother of soft hair falls across my face.

"Fuck!" says a voice in my ear, then with irritation, "Can't you watch out!" followed by a more concerned, "Are you all right?"

A small dog is running round and jumping over the two of us, its rope lead, the thing that must have tripped me, trailing behind. I take a closer at whoever has fallen with me. I know before I see her properly. Goldilocks.

"I'm OK," I say shakily. "What about you?"

I do seem to be all right apart from being winded for the second time that night. Though my ankle still hurts it didn't stop me running. I struggle to my feet and offer a hand to pull her up.

"Sorry. Didn't see you."

"'S'all right."

Her voice is a surprise. It is ... well, small, perhaps even a bit babyish. But what I really don't expect at all is the local accent, broad, almost peasant-like, far broader than Carol's. Low, Gran would have called it, and she wouldn't have meant low in volume.

"Ah!"

Standing with my help, she draws my superglued hand closer, peers closely at it. "You'm got a withered 'and."

The sympathy surprises me. Embarrassed, I try to pull away, but she holds on. It isn't the time or place to tell her the real story behind my misfortune, and a shout from not far behind alerts us again to the immediate peril. She calls softly to her dog.

"Lucy. Here girl."

The dog comes back to weave between our legs, and she clutches the trailing lead with her free hand while still not releasing mine.

"We must go," I say, but even as the words come out she is ahead of me, tugging.

"Come with me. I knows a way."

And she does, a tortuous path through thick bushes. We stop once and let gruff voices pass close while we crouch, holding our breaths, the dog diligently silent until they are gone. Then we press on. We emerge on one of the tiny paths through an area I recognise as the ornamental garden and progress some way along it before she again dives off to one side.

"Nearly there," she whispers huskily, keeping hold of me, as if I am another animal in her care. Perhaps seeing the disabled hand has made her want to do that?

Tall, spiked railings are now on one side of us, behind a cropped privet hedge, and just before the hedge comes to an end, we make another sudden lurch to one side and squeeze through a gap where one of the spear-like railings is missing. Suddenly we are on the close-cropped grass of the bowling green. We are just about to make a dash across the open ground when an awful groan comes through the darkness from not far away.

"Help, help, for God's sake help!"

Ballard's voice? We stop. I look over my shoulder. Because of the way the ground falls away behind them, the railings are in silhouette against the sky. We can see two figures, one perched on top of the railings, straddling them, and another a little further along, spreadeagled as if nailed to the iron spears. My mouth falls open: it looks just like the crucifixion.

"Did they hear us?" a shaky voice, surely Roy Selincourt's, drifts towards us.

There is another dreadful croak, this time from the spreadeagled figure. I shake off my guide's hand and start to move towards them. I think I recognise the other voice. Is it Ballard?

"Ballard?"

But the only answer is another groan.

"Come on," Goldilocks clutches my arm and hisses urgently. "Somebody'll find them. Come on!"

And she finds my hand again, pulls. I have to follow, albeit reluctantly.

121

She is certainly right that we should move on, for the park is being searched thoroughly by God knows how many policemen. And somebody will surely find the figures on the railings and help them whatever their predicament.

We hurry on across the bowling greens. We must look like strange chess pieces, me, her and the dog on the neat, manicured lines of grass. She expertly locates another gap in the railings on the far side and we slip through. We are now to my surprise back on the street, outside the park perimeter.

Both out of breath we nevertheless start to hurry back towards the town centre, still not feeling safe. All at once she checks.

"Look out!"

Two policemen have emerged from one of the small side-gates to the park not far ahead of us. She slips her arm through mine, draws me close.

"Walk like we're lovers," she hisses "They don't know we was in there."

Trying to look nonchalant and unaware of all that has passed in the last few minutes we walk on slowly towards the two figures as if we are out for a late stroll, giving the dog a last turn. They look closely at us. She nudges me to cross over the road before we reach them. Then, without warning, while we are under a street lamp, she pulls my head down and kisses me with warm little lips. It feels something like an electric shock. But this is no time to dawdle, and we move on calmly, as if we have all the time in the world.

They are still looking our way and I feel the hairs on my neck rise, but that kiss did the trick for them, I guess. Never mind what it did to me.

After that the policemen lose interest, and after a glance up and down the empty road the two head back through the gateway into the park.

Only when we turn off the park perimeter road into a side street do I feel really safe. Now we walk quicker to distance ourselves from the danger.

"I think we're OK now," I say in a bit, though I don't dare to look back. I feel her relax.

I look at her. She is much shorter than me. I think I have been trying not to look closely at her since that kiss.

It is impossible to tell the colour of her eyes, but they look blue, pale blue. She has a rather beautiful little face, lightly freckled. The glories of her tumbling copper hair have been turned dull grey by the street lighting.

She wears a knitted beret, crochet perhaps, with rings of different colours that are again transformed by the lighting, and a waisted sheepskin coat, with ragged bits of wool showing at the collar and cuffs. It's the sort of thing that was originally popular when Mum had been doing her hippie thing, judging by the photos and films of the time. She has washed-out flared jeans too, completing the picture. The overall effect is fetchingly waif-like. She would make a good poster for Les Misérables.

"Is it all right for you to take me 'ome?" she says suddenly.

"Sure. Where do you live?"

"No, your 'ome, silly. You got a place, 'aven't you?"

"I have, but..." I begin. Shall I tell her everything, now? It would take rather a long time.

"They locks me out," she says, downcast. "I got to go somewhere an' the cops'll be rounding up strays round town soon."

"All right," I say, feeling at the same time protective and alarmed at what our reception might be. "Come on."

At that moment the Town Hall clock starts to strike midnight.

Isn't it strange? I had her down as a sophisticated traveller, worldly wise and self-reliant and certainly a creature of some experience. But the strong local accent puts her somewhere else, and she is also quaintly ill-educated.

"I live with my Mum, and we'll have to make the best of it," I say to prepare her, adding, "but we'll be all right, I expect. What do you mean, you get locked out?"

"My step-dad, really. Mum's all right. I looks after her. We 'ave to look after each other."

I reflect that fathers might not be of the consistent quality I had long assumed them to be. Certainly they aren't all good.

"What, you mean he ... what?" Alarming things were forming in my head: was her father a drunkard? A wife-beater?

She shrugs, then confirms the impressions I have just gained of the man of the house.

"'E's all right really, 'cept when he's been on the drink. Then Mum says she 'opes e'll go away, or get put away."

Not so far off the mark then. And because of my recent obsession, I hear myself saying: "And have you lived here long? Your stepdad ... has he been with you a long time? What happened to your ... your real dad?"

"He died. I don't remember him much. I was only five. Sean's from Ireland. He only moved in five or six years ago. A hopeless Mick, my mum calls 'im."

She looks downcast again which makes me feel protective. "Not far to go now," I say to change the subject.

We finish most of the rest of the distance in silence. As we come round the last corner I remember the afternoon visit of the doctor, and I'm shocked it has all gone out of my head for so long. I hope Mum had had a peaceful evening. What, though, I wonder, will she make of this stranger I am bringing home? Can we perhaps get in without her seeing us? What will the dog do? Where will it sleep? We are not used to pets in our house, let alone overnighting women. If we wake Mum, will she applaud this all as evidence of a new spirit of adventure on my part? Will she want to talk? If she is awake of course she will, I realise. It is the first time I have ever brought anyone home this late at night, let alone to stay, let alone a figure so – well, rather romantic I suppose. Hell, I don't even know how I can begin to introduce Goldilocks. I don't even know her real name for a start. Better find that out fast, I think, as we make the final approach.

"By the way, I'm Pete..." I start clumsily.

"I know. I've seen you round. I'm Jane."

I can virtually hear Mum turning the name over: "Jane Eh? And where is Jane expecting to spend the night?"

"It's a nice name," I begin, turning into the gate. The house is in darkness.

"It's a shitty name and I don't like it. I want to change it. Call me Holly. Most do."

125

I don't pursue this further. I fit the key in the lock and turn it softly as I can, putting my finger to my lips.

"Quiet," I caution. "My mum's probably asleep. She's downstairs in the sitting room. She hasn't been well. Chest." I tap my chest. It doesn't seem the right moment to fill-in more details.

"Oh."

Where was Jane, or Holly, going to spend the night here? My bed seems the obvious answer. In a trice I make up my mind to be noble, make a sacrifice of it. There is still a single bed with a mattress in what we call Mum's bedroom, which is my former room. I could rough it on that with a blanket. Come to that, I can sleep on the floor in my own room while she has the bed. That decided, I put the problems aside.

Inside, all is silent, the sitting room door slightly ajar. I listen there for a moment with the girl and the dog hovering just inside the front door. Nothing. That is a relief. I pull the door to and, cautioning again for silence, I lead the way upstairs. We go into my bedroom and I shut the door, put on the light.

She pulls off her beret, sits on the bed, looks around. At a pointed command the dog slips silently under the bed and is quiet.

It has been a long time since anybody except me has even been in this room. Andrea Twaite has been in, once. I remember with embarrassment the pathetic fumblings, a rebuke. I also remember, suddenly, the painting and Mike Collins' critique, and an even deeper embarrassment eclipses the Andrea incident. Christ, I think, I hope she doesn't notice the stack in the corner, ask to look at them. The more I look round the room the more it

126

is full of traps. She might even ask me to play the guitar. God, how I hope that won't happen.

Instead, to my eternal relief, after giving her new surroundings a cursory look-over, she relaxes visibly. Unbuttoning her coat, she empties a handful of toffees from one of her pockets, takes a packet of Golden Virginia from the other along with matches and a packet of Rizla papers. Selecting one of the sweets she puts the rest back. She undoes the wrapper carefully, holds the contents up to her nose.

"Best Moroccan," she says with a quick, sly little smile.

I take off my jacket. I sit at my desk bemused, watching in silence as she expertly rolls a joint, cooking a corner of the square toffee-like tablet of hashish in a match flame and sending a curl of herbal-smelling smoke my way. She sets the rest of the little block of dope beside my bed.

Since spotty Mike Collins and his flashy Benson and Hedges nobody has smoked anything in this room, even in this house. I make no move to stop her, even when she lights up, takes a deep draw, holds it.

She exhales, smiles and holds the joint out so the butt points to me.

"It's good," she says. "Try some."

Of course, I have tried dope before. Tell me who hasn't. Some individuals, even whole groups come to that, took to it eagerly, and I knew users whose attitudes to it ranged from treating it as an occasional recreational drug to making it worthy of reverential awe, even worship. For myself, even if I could afford it, I could take it or leave it.

Dope of any kind had held no appeal for years now. I'd also taken a couple of Es some time ago, to no great effect other than losing some sleep, while crack and anything else like that frankly frightened me. But in this strange situation now I don't refuse. Perhaps there's nothing left to lose, except ... well, you know.

I intend to take a shallow, cautious inhalation, a 'Bill Clinton', but the joint is so well-made it draws easily and smoothly, and I feel the smoke filling my lungs without effort.

"See, it's all right, eh? I knows good stuff. I deals. You can buy some, if you want. Cost price. Just to try."

"You're a dealer?" I hunt round, suddenly anxious about what to do with the 'evidence' and find an old china painting palette for an ashtray.

"Sure. What about you? What do you do to stay alive?" She has the joint back now and lies back looking at the ceiling as she takes more deep pulls. Her coat falls open, showing her slight but nevertheless appealing figure in a navy T-shirt.

"Me? I'm on the dole. I don't really know what I want to do. Where do you deal?"

She sits up again, joint in her mouth, and pushes off the coat, letting it fall back on the bed. She squints at me with one quizzical eye, which is indeed light blue. It's as if I am being measured.

"All over town, students mostly," she says. "I knows what I wants. I'm saving up. I'm getting a hairdressers, for mum and me. For when 'e goes, the 'opeless mick. Mum says e'll end up in jail soon anyway."

I can't match the image I have of her with this concept of future bliss as a hair stylist, but I'm warming to her honesty and the homeliness of her ambitions, juxtaposed as they were with her lawless employment and her appearance as an exotic bohemian adventuress.

"You're very quiet," she says, still scrutinising me. "You want to relax, you know. Here..."

She passes the dwindling joint back to me. "And show me the lav. I'm dying for a pee."

I open the door and point the way, and the dog suddenly emerges and pads silently after her. Then I do relax for a moment. My room smells of dog, dope and patchouli. But I start to feel OK with all this, a weight lifting from my shoulders.

I know I can let it all drop now, that fear of Mum making things difficult, for she is clearly fast asleep. I put her out of mind, so there's only the two of us, talking late in the night, in my head, everything else for the moment totally out of mind: the disastrous football match, the horrid Indian girls, Carol and Toby, Glynnis, Ballard's amazing revelations, the wake by the lake and the fiasco that followed, and our reckless escape. Even, eventually, poor old Mum downstairs. Nothing seems to matter any more. There is nothing that won't wait until morning. I hear the town clocks striking one. It seems an age after that when she returns with the dog, smelling of soap and toothpaste, but looking at the bedside clock I see just a few minutes have passed. I suddenly feel very tired.

I must go to the loo too. I take a good long hard look at myself in the shaving mirror. Red eyes, face a little bit puffy, otherwise OK. When I get back, she has picked her coat off the bed and has put it on my desk.

"We should sleep," she says, starting to undress. The dog dives back under the bed.

"I'll go ... other room," I mumble, moving towards the door. By this time, she is down to her T-shirt and knickers. She slips under my covers and holds up a corner of the duvet.

"Come on, don't just stand there," she says. "Don't be daft."

And she gives me a wide and beautiful grin.

Chapter 10 Own goal

You know how you can sometimes vividly picture things you would like to happen to you, things you haven't yet experienced? With full details of the circumstances, the setting? Well, I do, anyway, but I never imagined it happening this way, certainly not since my frustrated fumbling with Andrea Twaite. Perhaps I could imagine something like this happening in the park, in the dark, with Glynnis or Carol. Already in a day I have become remarkably fickle! Yes, love in the park would be suitably romantic. But not here, with my sick mother downstairs and in my own bed, with a dog underneath us. You couldn't make that up.

I wonder briefly if I should find pyjamas, but that would take too long to organise even if it was wise. Instead, I opt to keep on my underpants. And I put out the bedside light to strip with modesty, and perhaps ashamed that the sight of my puny physique in my underwear will spoil everything. Then I climb into bed, desperately trying not to touch any part of her. I have to say 'sorry' a lot because this endeavour not actually possible. I try the best I can though, which leaves me balancing on the edge of the bed, half in and half out, scared to move. A giggle. Then fingertips touch me, followed by a hand. Her other arm snakes out round my neck.

It is an encounter with few words. To my complete surprise no instructions are necessary; our remaining bits of clothing come off and get pushed out of the bed. Her kissing, fierce at first, becomes by degrees gentler. At one stage we unlock, and she slips out of bed and away to her coat. She returns opening a small packet. A condom.

"We don't need..." I start to mumble.

She takes no notice and guides me expertly. Is she thinking I might find it difficult because of what she thinks is a withered hand?

"Better 'ad," she says, business-like. "We'd spend a month or so worried about it elsewise, and maybe even the rest of our lives after that."

"Eh? What?"

"No matter." And another giggle. "You 'aven't done this before, 'ave you?"

And that is the end of nearly a quarter century of build-up. Oh lord, it relegates squalid onanism to at least a million leagues down. I forget my three very old imaginary friends in an instant, cast out, never to return, I hope.

At some point we stop and smoke another joint. From time to time too there is a crossover into unconsciousness, always followed by a waking need.

It is in one of these times adrift that the football game comes back. Only this time I am part of it, I am actually on the field.

The whole country has been holding its breath for this game, I know.

Now the road to Shizuoka, for me and most non-football-following Brits, really started back in September, when we beat Germany. It was as joyous as it was unexpected, touching some deep national feelings through traditional rivalries, on and off the football pitch. And what a win it was - Germany 1, England 5.

"It's coming home," people started to say, "Football's coming home..."

From about May, competition had become intense. By this stage the crucial games were being hosted in Japan, with the coveted final, the last drama, set to be played Yokohama. English fans following their heroes from game to game, a notoriously rowdy bunch with a bad reputation for trouble, had managed to put on their best behaviour. There were no drunken riots, everything was friendly, relaxed, and as we approached the crunch match with Brazil everyone at home in England was rooting for our side. St George's flags flew everywhere, full sized ones from pubs and buildings and dangling out of house windows, little ones jigging and flicking in the wind on car and lorry aerials. Shops and stores had sold out of them; even home-made ones had started to appear. For the last few days, a carnival atmosphere had been gripping the entire country.

"It's Coming Home," echoed the radio non-stop, sounding confident, almost triumphal. And people sang along with any number of other gung-ho football ditties pumping out on the airwaves. People who had never watched a football game before, or who knew or cared very little about it, had become enthusiasts, experts in gameplay and tactics and shrewd judges of the abilities of a wide range of players from many countries.

And tonight of all nights here I am, with Beckham et al, in Shizuoka. I mean I'm actually dreaming I'm there, as part of the England team!

With the rest of the team I walk out to cheers in a grand stadium boasting the last word in technology. The Japanese can even lift the entire pitch and truck it out of the stadium on rollers for groundsmen to look after it.

We need rain, I know. Earlier that week it had rained. Rain suits England. Rain is our national playing medium. But there isn't a cloud in the sky: Beckham has his head on one side, looking up, frowning. It is hot, very hot. However, we are fresh, for a while at least we think we can cope. We start to limber up. Beckham, with his currently crested hairdo, notices me and smiles. He passes the ball to me, just a nudge, and I tap it back. He passes it on to someone next to me, and so it continues, the ball going from Beckham to player after player. We are near the subs benches and when I look over there is our manager, Eriksson, pacing, tense. I jog over for a closer look, but he continues to stare at the ground, preoccupied, pulling on his chin. I want to tell him not to worry but I cannot catch his eye.

A whistle blows. There is a sudden ripple of expectation through the crowd. We are ready to start. The formations line up. There are shouts for England, shouts for Brazil. Apart from our own fans, thousands have travelled to see the game. Many Japanese spectators have swung behind us, even to the extent of having their faces greasepainted with a broad white cross on red, for England, Beckham and St George! Beckham looks round his team. He seems to be happy with my left midfield position.

Apart from Seaman, Beckham and me, we have fielded Danny Mills, Sol Campbell, Rio Ferdinand, Ashley Cole, Paul Scholes, Nicky Butt, Trevor Sinclair, Michael Owen and Emile Heskey; on the subs' bench with Sven are Wayne Bridge, Wes Brown, Joe Cole, Keiron Dyer, Robbie Fowler, Owen Hargreaves, David James, Martin Keown, Nigel Martyn, Teddy Sheringham, Gareth Southgate and Darius Vassell. We face Marcos, Roque Junior, Lucio, Edmilson, Cafu, Gilberto, Ronaldinho, Kleberson, Roberto Carlos, Ronaldo and Rivaldo.

They look mean, quick, and above all at ease; their banter is like quicksilver, incomprehensible. This makes them much worse, much more dangerous.

If there is a whistle, I don't hear it, but all of a sudden, we are moving forward.

Before many minutes pass Ashley Cole has a chance at goal, but the Brazilians push it over the line for a corner in our favour. Positive, that feels. A great start. I hang back outside the penalty box while Beckham sends an inswinger, but infuriatingly it is punched away by goalie Marcos for a throw-in.

So far so good. We're doing OK. I seem to have no immediate role, but I do appear to be the only unmarked player on the pitch. Perhaps it is my job to fill empty spaces, deter any passes that might go through them. I watch Roque Junior foul Owen on the line; good, that means a penalty for us.

Beckham takes the kick. It goes to Heskey who speeds it on its way, only to find Marcos's hands again. Damn!

"C'mon England!" I suddenly hear Mum's voice from the crowd. I look over, and there she is, waving, on her feet, excited. She looks years younger.

"Give it to them!" she shouts, smiling specially at me. I look down proudly to see the three little lions, our emblem, on my chest. Then I turn to concentrate on the game. It seems to be running on rather familiar lines, though the perspective is a little strange. It is many years since I played soccer, but for the moment that's no worry.

Good job I look up at this point; after sailing over my head in the clear bright Shizuoka sky the ball makes its way to Ronaldo, their key player, and although he is 30 yards off goal the danger is clear. He has space in front of him – I am not doing my job, and it is time to swing into action. But even as I make up the ground he lets fly. I let go of my breath with relief when the ball shoots wide of goal.

Despite constant challenges I feel England are going great guns, me especially. I can move rapidly to any part of the pitch with scarcely any effort. It is as if I have winged boots. I don't even feel too warm, let alone hot.

"C'mon England! C'mon Pete!"

More familiar voices. I look round. Glynnis and Carol are in the front row, faces painted like tribal warriors, each holding on to separate ends of a red and white scarf which they have stretched high above them, waving it like a banner. Pride surges again, only to be marred somewhat when this amicable situation deteriorates and each girl tries to tear the scarf away from the other, spite on both faces.

But I have to turn my attention back to the game. Just in time. We seem to have run into a bit of bother. Carlos has just made a long throw in, and Rivaldo is racing towards our penalty area to intercept with a high chance of striking for goal. It is a race between him and Seaman. But Seaman collects it safely, just as I somehow knew he would. I can breathe again.

Then it is our turn. Up front, Nicky Butt gets a good pass through to Scholes. At 25 yards it is worth a shot. Once again someone is in the way, Lucio, I think.

"Sod!" exclaims a voice beside me. I look up to find it is my former friend and art critic Mike Collins, spots and all, running beside me. He looks more than a little unfit. How come he has made the team?

"You know, goals are a bit like fannies, aren't they?" he puffs. "Hard to get a shot at them and then there's always some other bastard bloke standing in the way."

To my relief he jogs off, panting horribly, to join the defence: Scholes has now fouled Ronaldinho, and Carlos is coming up for a free kick. Our defence wall is quickly lined up, Mike Collins disappearing among them. How true, I think, reflecting on Mike's philosophical remark about fannies. And sometimes there's a lot of people standing in the way, I think. And then I think of something smart to say back to him when I get a chance: sometimes they're like buses – none for a long time then many appearing all at once.

Carlos puts in a ripping penalty shot and you can almost hear it humming through the air, but our defence wall stands firm, and it is deflected for a corner. A collected groan goes up from the crowd, cheated of having at least one goal on the scoreboard.

What follows is a lot of dangerous dithering in our goal mouth. There are two more corners. Silva and Ronaldo both have chances. Ronaldo is a persistent troublemaker.

But somehow, we manage to survive and slowly the action moves back up the field. Mills then passes to Heskey, and a rhythm begins to develop. Heskey is looking for Michael Owen and sends the ball on its way but their defence pounces. Not quickly enough though. Owen snatches back control and turns on the goal to fire. For once the unlucky Marcos dives the wrong way!

Is it a goal? Can it be true? An England goal?

Everything erupts. We have a goal! Just 23 minutes into the game and we are one up! The stadium roar is deafening; I know that back at home in every pub and club in the country, probably in every home too, people are on their feet, yelling like wild things. The infamous Tap will surely be in uproar.

I anxiously scan the sea of faces in the crowd, looking for someone I know so I can share this triumph with them, but it is impossible to recognise anyone I know now. Mum, Carol and Glynnis have been lost in a sea of people.

As for the Brazilians, they are a bit annoyed to say the least. But that doesn't mean they let their heads fall; far from it. From a few wry grins over this setback, their faces set to masks of resolve. We are for it, we know. This is war. The whole mood and tempo of the game has changed the instant we scored.

First casualty of the inevitable retaliation is Beckham. He bounces away from a tussle with Ronaldo and falls, clutching his ankle. A gasp runs round the stadium. I jog closer to look. His face is white with pain. Along with millions of other Britons I am willing him to rub it, get over it, get up. Our other players are standing round, anxious. The medicine man rushes on, starts checking him over. To collected dismay he shakes his head. A stretcher is called for, and suddenly we are without a captain. I am not the only one, player or fan, with a sinking feeling in the stomach.

Luckily it is a short-lived disappointment. After a scant minute there is a huge roar from the crowd, unconnected with the state of play. I look round and see to my delight that Beckham is back, running onto the field smiling. Faces light up across our team. We are back in business.

At this stage the game becomes more finely balanced, neither side in complete control. Play moves in waves from one end of the field to the other and back, with competent challenges on both goals. But then Seaman leaps high to meet a challenge from Rivaldo, clutches the ball but falls heavily, his neck and back touching ground first. There is a sickening thump and what sounds like the crunch of shattered bone. Oh no, I think, he's broken his back. Or his neck. Oh my God no! Surely he can't escape from a fall like that without a bad injury? For a moment or two he seems unconscious. A hush falls over the crowd. The medics come on again. Knots of players stand about in little groups surveying the scene. There is deep worry on their faces.

"Christ, looks like they're going to kill us all!"

I look round. This time the voice in my ear comes from Alan Jones. He's another player I can't remember seeing when we kicked off.

"I'm fucking off Walker. These fuckers are mad. I don't want to die. Are you coming?"

He lets his shiny thick bottom lip drop, turns his back and starts to walk off the field. Typical, I think. Who needs someone like you on their side?

Luckily Seaman isn't dead. He is just winded, as anyone would be after such a fall, and evidently sore. He sits up, rubs his back, and then stands with a little help, stretches himself. He is going to play on! The relief for us is mighty, as it must be for Seaman himself. What is more, half-time is in sight and before we know it we are playing in injury time.

But just as the minutes draw out towards that tantalising whistle I watch with horror as a damaging drama unfolds. Ronadinho rushes past Scholes and draws Campbell out of position, then slips the ball to Rivaldo who picks it up with a left footed shot. So smooth, so fluid, the whole fucking move. It sort of sneaks past Seaman and into the corner of the net.

With one blow we are level, even stevens, and the precious advantage that entering half time one-up would have given us has slipped away.

So we are disappointed when the whistle blows. But hey, nobody is actually winning, are they?

Seaman finds me in the interval. I am standing alone because I don't really know anyone else. Mike Collins seems to have vanished, Jones too for the moment. Our goalie is rubbing his back.

"Does it hurt?" I ask.

He grimaces. "A bit. How's your mum?"

"Fine thanks. Much better, that is. She's in the crowd. Didn't you see her?"

He shakes his head.

"You know her?"

"Everyone knows your mum. She's a great kid."

"Everyone? Really?"

"Sure. Everyone."

He puts a gloved hand on my shoulder. I flinch a bit, somehow knowing those hands are hard, strong. They are surprisingly gentle.

"Look, I know what you're thinking..."

He speaks with sincerity.

"It isn't me. Anyway, it's no big deal having a dad, you should know that. Now come on, let's see if we can win. This isn't going to be so easy."

With a final comforting pat and smile he is off, and we are heading out into the field of dreams again.

We start the second half well enough, which is good because we need to. Rouque Junior downs Heskey and we win a free kick. Beckham comes up to take it. He sets up a header for Owen, but I watch with dismay as it sails over the bar.

Then Brazil wins a free kick from a hard challenge by Scholes on Kleberson. I view the move with gloom. The spot is 40 yards off goal but it means Brazil can bring everyone into a challenging position. Ronaldinho lines up his shot.

Like everyone else I expect him to send it up for his players in the penalty box but instead it sails high and true, bound for the open goal mouth. Keeper Seaman, miles out of goal, watches it float over his head. The ball dips ominously. It enters the net unhindered. Even Ronadinho can hardly believe his eyes from the look on his face.

Now we really have a mountain to climb.

Fatigue, the heat and now this new setback are starting to affect us badly, even though we keep out the next 30-yard free kick from Cafu. Eriksson decides Trevor Sinclair could come off the flank and a fresh Kieron Dyer takes his place.

Then the ref sends off Ronaldinho; a red card for raising his studs while challenging Mills. It is a hard and perhaps a wrong decision, but I feel hope rising. They are now down to 10 players, while we not only have a full team but apparently have a few novice extras like me and Mike Collins and Jones floating in and out of the game.

However, with the game in its final quarter the Brazilians start to do their best to kill time and starve us out, winding down the clock. And we are a spent force for all our numbers, although Mills has a shot. The pacing Eriksson makes another substitute, putting in Darius Vassell and Teddy Sheringhham in place of Ashley Cole and Owen, but the move smacks of desperation.

Only in the dying minutes do I feel things picking up for us again. We force a corner, Beckham takes it. Butt heads it wide.

But wait, it isn't quite over. Beckham, racing in, saves the loose ball from going over the line, and in an instant I can see he has a good chance. He can see it too, and has his foot raised to strike when he catches my eye.

Which is when I realise why I am there. Instead of unleashing his shot he slows down, taps the ball gently at me.

"It's your turn now, Pete," he says. "Make it a good one."

And the ball is at my feet, the goal open wide in front of me.

Which is a hell of a time to wake up, I think you'll agree.

Chapter 11 Disaster

I am alone when I wake, but it doesn't surprise me. As I come slowly back to my senses the disappointment of not knowing how my goal shot for England might have gone lingers for some moments. However, it is soon replaced by a languorous feeling of well-being, better even than yesterday's waking moments. The feeling intensifies as the events of last evening start to drift back into my head.

The new day is flooding the room with light. It is half past eight, just gone. I am completely naked. There is no Goldilocks, no dog, no coat. But I do not doubt she has been here. That was not a dream. She and her faithful companion must have left without waking me, for the house is quiet, at peace. Yet I can also hear no coughing. I feel myself smiling. I lie still looking at the ceiling for some time and do my best to relive it all. It was all ... well, quite thrilling, I suppose. And my body feels different, new. I know now it is capable of some surprising things.

I remember the condom; leaning over and looking under the bed I discover two, both untied and covered in whippet hair. Am I really that productive? God, that is good, isn't it? Everything works! I probe with my toes for my pants only to locate another discarded rubber. Even better! That really is quite some progress. I sit up, roll out of bed and pad to the bathroom where I manage to flush the evidence away after two or three goes, trying not to pull the flush too violently for fear of waking Mum. I can't think what else I can do with them.

Then I run a bath, making it a big one with a dollop of cheap bubbly bath essence. I often have a bath like this at weekends before going downstairs, and this time as always I try to keep it quiet for Mum's sake. I lie steaming in the deep water for some time, happy in my revised state of being. When I return to my room to dress I see Goldliocks has left some other presents. There is a liquorish toffee wrapper by the clock and a neatly rolled joint. This makes me smile.

I find clean underwear and a new T-shirt, jeans and runners and my cotton jacket. I pocket the bedside gifts. The joint goes gently into the breast pocket. Then I go downstairs, still feeling mighty good.

I push Mum's door gently open, trying to make sure that grin of triumph that is trying to burst out is reined back. No sound. I go over to the dark shape of her on the couch and reach out to shake her shoulder gently.

But all I feel is unyielding rigidity. Although my shocked mind cannot quite accept the fact I realise she will never ever wake again.

The very first thing that flashes into my head after it all sinks in is the last time I came down with flu, real flu, and Mum saying if anything is going to go wrong it will always happen at the weekend, when you can't get hold of anyone, when it is most awkward. Sod's law. A damn funny thought at such a time, but nevertheless apt in its own way.

Nobody can be fully prepared for moments like this. I go quickly to the window, pull the curtains back to let some light in, then return. She has a half smile on her face, that smile, her eyes a little open as if she is still alive. I reach out to feel her face, her skin. It is cool but not really cold, like I expect. The stillness makes me pull my hand away again. I see the panic button around her neck and I pick it up and press it hard, then again and again, without thinking clearly about what I am doing. It seems to me after some moments the damn thing is not working, for nobody has rushed to my aid, and I reach for the phone and dial 999. My hands are shaking. A girl's voice answers. She asks for the telephone number and then which service I want. I am not sure what I want. What service should you call for a dead person? When she asks again, I say, "I think my mum's dead," and she says she will send an ambulance. But then when she asks again for our telephone number I cannot remember it. I know I'm panicking, not being rational. Eventually the number comes back into my head, and she asks me to stand in the street to show the ambulance crew where to stop. I put the phone down. I pick it up again immediately and call Doctor Cohen, using the number on the card he has left by Mum's bed.

The clinic is closed, of course, and theree's a recorded message, so I try the home number which the card says is for emergencies only. There's a little wait and I feel panicky again but then Dr Cohen answers the phone himself and when I tell him what has happened he says he will be round right away. Am I all right, he asks? "I'm OK," I say, immediately knowing it sounds silly, "I already called for an ambulance."

Then I go back to Mum and wonder if I should be trying to give her heart massage, or mouth to mouth resuscitation, although I am not quite sure how to do either. But she looks very peaceful and I feel I should not disturb her. At the same time, I am desperately wishing she would wake, yawn, stretch.

I leave her again and go back to the window and look up and down the street. It is empty apart from parked cars. I pace for a while between her and the window and then, exasperated, I go to the front door and out to the gate to look the ambulance from there. This feels wrong too, so I go back in, which is no good either, so I come out again. It develops into a routine, in and out and then, suddenly, there is an ambulance, lights flashing and siren wailing. It sounds like, "*Oh no! Oh no! Oh no!*", and it is turning into our street but moving really slowly. Why is it moving so slowly? Are they looking for door numbers? I run out into the road where the driver can se me and wave furiously with both arms in the air. I'm conscious other people are looking out of their windows, from behind curtains. It draws up by me and two people in green overalls, a man and a woman, jump out. I can't say anything, words just won't come, but I point to to the door and they go in, me following. As I find my voice and shout after them: "In the sitting room. Turn left," I am vaguely aware of another vehicle pulling up. It is Dr Cohen's car.

Then I go back inside and a paramedic is kneeling by Mum and feeling her neck. The woman is on a mobile phone talking to someone.

"Is she dead?"

I already know the answer.

"She's been gone for some time." He has a gentle voice, but matter of fact, and I realise he is not talking just to me but to someone behind me as well. A hand rests on my shoulder.

"Did you find her, Peter?" Dr Cohen's voice.

Suddenly I am unable to stem a flood of tears or escape a sudden sense of wretchedness – breaking down, I suppose you would call it. Hands help me to a chair.

At the end of this spasm I look up to see the doctor dismissing the two paramedics.

"Is he going to be all right?" The skinny woman who is the other part of the crew says with a nod in my direction. She is very matter of fact too, like her partner. It's a job.

"I'll see to it. Don't worry."

They go.

The doctor has a frown of concern.

"I'm sorry, Peter. There's nothing we can do. But it does look as if she went peacefully. Were you asleep most of the night?"

"When? When did she ... go?"

I hear my voice as if it is coming from somewhere else rather than from me, somewhere remote and unconnected.

"Some time ago, I would say. Before midnight perhaps. I don't think you could have helped even if you had been with her. You mustn't blame yourself."

If I am going to blame myself for not being beside her when it happened it is too early yet. Instead, I am still desperately trying to think all this isn't real, it isn't happening, it is some horrible dream.

But it is not a dream, I know deep down.

Chapter 12 Dark days

Dr Cohen sits opposite me. On the couch, Mum's face has been covered and I can see no other part of her, just the shape under the duvet. I can't stop myself starting to sob again.

"I'm sorry," the doctor says. "Look, is there someone we can contact? Relatives? You're an only son, aren't you, but did your mother have a sister? A brother? Aunts, uncles, that sort of thing? Is your father still alive? Do you know..."

He tails off, seeing the answers are written my face. There is not any other relative. We were just a unit, Mum and me. Our last living relative, so far as I know, was Gran. I shake my head.

"No. No dad. Just us," I manage to say.

"Close friends, then?"

"No. She had friends, but not close. Nobody we saw a lot. Nobody who can help."

"Your friends, I mean. What about you? Why don't you call a girlfriend? I'm sure she'll help."

I think first that I haven't got a girlfriend, and I know immediately that it is not quite true now, not after yesterday.

"No," I say, pulling myself together. "Not now. I'm all right. I'll call them ... her ... later."

But a wave of loss suddenly dents my confidence and I once again dissolve in tears. Dr Cohen gets up and puts a comforting hand on my shoulder again.

"I'm sorry," I sob.

"It's all right don't worry. It's all perfectly natural, grief, and you will learn to live with it in time. But I can see it's a shock for you. I can give you something to take for that, but it's better to let it out. Tea would help though. Will you be all right here for a minute if I make some? In the kitchen ... is it easy to find?"

I nod, pointing my arm in the direction of the kitchen and realising with a shock that my hand is still glued shut.

"Good lad. I'll make some tea then we'll try to sort something out. Absolutely no need to worry though, no need at all. I'll be back in a minute."

Like probably everyone else of my age I do not go around thinking of the inevitability of death, particularly for myself, yet now I'm alone the unmoving shape on the couch is its proof, the reality. I want to see Mum again, but I cannot bring myself to go over to her. I am rooted in my seat, from where I listen to the sounds of the doctor making tea. He comes back with two drinks. One of them is in her favourite mug, but he isn't to know that. My good hand shakes as I take that cup from him. I have to put it down quickly.

He picks up the phone.

"If you don't mind me using your phone, I'll call Social Services, though it's a devil of a job to get hold of anyone on a Saturday. Who was Mum's home help? She had a nurse, didn't she?"

"Tania Watson. She's from Macmillans, not Social Services."

He gets through almost immediately, talks briefly and then puts the phone down.

"Lucky – there's someone in. They're sending a counsellor who'll help you with things. And they're contacting Mrs

149

Watson. She may come over after her rounds, they seem to think. I'll just hang on a bit longer, if you like."

"Please."

We both sit while the tea goes cold. He at least has something to do, first scribbling some notes then filling out a form. He bobs up and places the sheet of paper on Mum's bedside table, propped up against her still half-full glass of water, then sits again.

"That's a very important note. You'll need it, so don't lose it. In time you will have to get a certificate from the registrar, but leave that for now. There may be an inquest, but I would think not."

"Inquest?"

"Yes. The coroner must be informed, but it's usually just a formality. Sometimes they do an autopsy too. Mum was quite ill and there's a history of that, so they maybe won't bother. I've just recorded that her heart stopped. Probably the pulse got weak, myocardia, but if she was sleeping she wouldn't really know. Certainly no pain, you can be sure. How are you feeling now?"

"OK I guess."

At this point I actually do begin to feel a little bit more in control of myself. But all the same an underlying sense of desolation comes and goes, like waves breaking on a beach. I try to tell the doctor how I feel.

"That's good. Shock can make you feel pretty unwell, so if you do have any problems at all call me at once. It should pass though, but you could find things strange for some time. I'd call your friends soon, too, your girlfriend most of all. And try to get

150

out if you can, if only for a few minutes. It helps if you're able to change your perspective."

"Go out? Leave Mum you mean?"

"No. After. The funeral people will come and take her away soon, help you to make arrangements. She wasn't a churchgoer, was she?"

I had not yet thought of a funeral. The word brought another wave of woe, but I pushed it back.

"We didn't ever go to church. Except once or twice, I remember, usually on Christmas eve."

"No matter. Everything will be all right. Really."

I stand and go to the window. The once familiar street seems alien, bleak. In the distance a man in a tweed jacket is hurrying our way from the direction of town, looking at house numbers. Somehow, I know he is looking for us. Sure enough, he stops at the gate, scans the front of the house. Perhaps he is trying to find some sign, some overt sign of death.

"Somebody's here."

The doctor nods and I go to the door.

The visitor is bearded, with large rather thick glasses, and a smile I first imagine is insincere but then I realise he is probably quite nervous. He is ten or so years older than me, I would say, but bearing in mind my recent preoccupations he is not at all old enough to be my dad. If ever I need a dad, it is now.

"Mr Walker?" he says, holding out a hand. "Brian Phillips, Social Services. I understand you've suffered a bereavement, Mr Walker. My sincere condolences at losing your wife."

"Mum. My mum," I correct him.

"Oh dear, I seem, to have the wrong information. My apologies."

More like he has drawn the wrong conclusions. There is an awkward moment on the doorstep when neither of us knows quite what to say, but then I find myself saying "come in" at exactly the moment he asks if he can step over the threshold.

I lead him back to the room where Dr Cohen is now standing, obviously anxious to be off. The newcomer introduces himself.

"Everything in order?" he says.

Doctor Cohen nods.

"I think so. Can you take care of Mr Walker - Peter? He's had quite a shock. You'll be able to tell him everything he needs to know?"

The man nods more times than is necessary.

I accompany Doctor Cohen to the door. I am about to shut it after him when he turns and says: "I'd try not to drink too much, eh? Alcohol, I mean. It doesn't always help. A bit perhaps but be careful."

My new visitor, Brian Phillips, is briskly efficient and as time passes, I warm to him. He has a cool head and is obviously no stranger to this sort of situation. He takes away the cold tea cups and makes some fresh, a potful, bringing in clean cups and a jug of milk too. Like the doctor he asks about churches, then asks whether I prefer a particular funeral director. I don't know any of course. He recommends the Co-op.

"They're very competitive," he says. "I think you'll find their rates are easily the best around. Up to you of course. We can ask for anyone you like. Shall I try the Co-op?"

"Now you mean?"

He makes the telephone call without answering me, ending it with what I think is an inappropriately cheerful 'bye'.

"They'll be here soon," he says. "They are very good. Just let them help you all they can. That's what they do best. You'll need that worry out of the way because there's quite a bit to do, I'm afraid, if you're up to it?"

I nod again, not quite taking in what he is saying. Another wave of grief starts to shake me. I look over to the covered shape on the sofa and tears well in my eyes. That is Mum, that shape. Surely in a moment she will wake up? And all this will be a dream...

He pours tea for us both and comes over with it, going back to sit himself where the doctor has been. He waits without looking at me directly until my sobs subside.

"I'd drink the tea if I were you," he says when I'm under control again. "You'll find it helps. We'll wait until they come before we get on with things. Take your time. At least you're lucky you didn't get caught up in all the shenanigans in the park last night. Have you heard about it?"

I'm silent. I can't immediately think what he is talking about. He continues.

"A rave, it seems. Lots of riotous behaviour, terrible things. The police had to break it up. Even reading the Riot Act, some say."

Memories of last night flood back. My glued hand gives a sudden twitch. I have been keeping it out of sight, either behind my back or deep in my pocket.

"What sort of terrible things?"

153

He looks glad he has managed to divert me, albeit temporarily.

"Well, you know what young people get up to. Lots of arrests. And there's talk of somebody being crucified. Actually crucified! Can you believe it in a town like this? It'll be in the paper, perhaps on television. Seems it started with all that early drinking because of the football match, you know, the World Cup. You know we lost? Shame. Are you interested in football?"

"It wasn't such a bad game, for all that," I hear myself saying.

And here at last, as we sit together and wait for the undertakers to come and collect Mum, I find I can go over the game blow by blow with this perfect stranger, a day late and a long way from the certainties of existence I was enjoying 24 hours ago.

We are deep in our recollections of the big match when there is a knock. Phillips leaves me sitting and goes to the door, returning with two men in black Melton overcoats who know just what a body looks like hidden under duvets and are clearly well able to judge they will need no additional help with this one, weight-wise. The elder of the two has thinning grey hair combed straight back, a sharp nose, a red and weathered complexion and a bowed back. He shakes hands with me. He has enormous hands.

"How d'you do? Mr Stapleton, at your service. My sincere condolences, Mr Walker. We'll take care of everything, of course."

Breezy. His companion, built as the colloquial saying goes 'like a brick shithouse', round-faced and equally red, crosses the room to Mum and for the first time I notice he is carrying a black canvas stretcher. Almost before I know it is happening, he rolls the blurry outline of the so familiar figure that has been with me all my life out of its covers and into the dark and enveloping confines of the carryall. Stapleton joins him in one pace and grabs one set of handles and they are off in one smooth movement towards the door.

"We'll be in touch, Mr Walker," says Stapleton "Our Mr Petal will probably call on you." And then they are gone as suddenly as they arrived.

I want to spring to the window and watch them take her out and away, but Brian Phillips checks me, gently urges me sit back down.

"There, there. I'm sorry. It has to happen."

Another massive sea-green wave rises and crashes on grey shingle. She has gone, she has left our house forever. She has also left with her secrets intact, the identity of my father along with the guilty secret of that dreadful murder in the desert.

I feel more alone than I have ever felt before. I have been conscious for some time that we were quite a small organisation, she and I, in the face of the world and compared with a lot of other families, but somehow while she was alive, she had been big enough to make up for all this. I not only feel very alone but very, very small and helpless.

I come out of my grey chasm again. My new minder is patting me on the shoulder.

"It's all right," he says. "It's OK, it's perfectly natural to feel this way. I understand. It's hard to take, but it will get better, believe me. People lose their dear ones all the time. That might

155

not help you now, but it will in time. We must go on living. Take heart."

He makes some more tea, and when we settle down he asks about home ownership and savings and insurance. Although I don't really feel right about it I invade the biscuit tin where I know she kept all the important papers; since her move downstairs it has lived in the sideboard, not her dressing table where it was kept before she got ill. We gently explore the contents together. There is a building society pass book with about £6,000 recorded, the house deeds, no insurance I can find, and a bundle of letters tied with a ribbon. I do not open these, but I note the top envelope has her name and our address on it, handwritten, the ink slightly faded. Nothing else seems of any consequence ... bills, receipts, guarantees, that sort of thing. A little black leather address book. Nothing that looks like a will. I sort of expect there should be one, with an old-fashioned script title on the outside "*The last will and testament...*" with a red wax seal. But no.

"At least you don't have any financial worries. There's ample to cover funeral expenses here."

Brian Phillips' voice brings me back. He is looking at the savings book. "Do you own the house? Was the mortgage paid, I mean, if you have one?"

"I don't know. I'm not sure."

I really didn't know. If Mum had ever told me anything about the matter, I could not remember what she had said. In silence we pack things back in the tin, including the letters.

"Do you think you can manage all the funeral business? I mean, the undertakers will do virtually everything, but they'll want your approval. If there's no religious ceremony involved you can have a simple service at the crematorium. She never said if she wanted to be cremated or anything?"

I remember a far distant holiday in Cornwall, a pretty inland valley with a distant view of the sea, a peaceful spot where we sat for a picnic on a sunny day. She'd said then it was a place she would like to be laid to rest. There was nothing about burial or ashes. As I tell this to Brian Phillips the tears start flooding back.

"There you are then," he says. "With cremation you can do that. You can scatter her ashes there. Do you think she would like that?"

At that moment there is another knock on the door and the question must be left unanswered. It is Tania.

The somewhat formal relationship has always existed between Tania and me, so it is a big surprise when she draws me into her ample bosom and pats my back.

"There, there," she croons. "My poor boy. I am so sorry."

Then she holds me back from her with both arms, studies my face for a moment before releasing me.

"God is merciful. I will make us some tea," she announces.

I tell her there is some already made but she looks down scornfully at the tray and its untouched cups with skin already forming on them.

"Fresh!" she says emphatically, heading for the kitchen, adding over her shoulder: "I have told the vicar. He is coming round."

It looks as though God is going to be in on it whether or not anyone wants. God of the desert people, I reflect, Yahweh. Not everything that goes on in the desert is merciful, I now know.

Although I have just been telling Brian Phillips of our self-excommunication, I let the vicar's announced arrival pass without comment. Phillips himself remains silent throughout Tania's visit, other than to say hello and goodbye.

She brings back tea and more biscuits, starts discretely gathering into a Tesco plastic carrier bag all the nursing paraphernalia and the pill rations still lying about, now and again looking at me and throwing a "There, there." The gathering-up has a practised air about it. She must have performed the act many times in many places.

When she has finished, she gives my arm a final squeeze and goes towards the door.

"Well, I will let myself out. If there's anything I can do, let me know."

She goes. Duty done; I think I might never see her again. God is merciful? She means it is a merciful release, I suppose. Her rounds undoubtedly take her into worse situations. Earth is not a great place for angels, who come in many shapes and sizes I am beginning to realise.

Now it is Brian Phillips' turn to rise, ask if I feel I can manage, wonder if he can call anyone for me. He passes me a card, says I should call him whenever I feel the need.

"I'll be fine," I say, and this time I really feel I will. Another one with their duty done, I think as I let him out after a final handshake.

The phone is ringing as I come back.

158

It is Roger Stenton. He has already heard the news of Mum's death. It is probably going round town like wildfire by now.

"I'm sorry," he says, adding a hanging query, "Was it...?"

"She died peacefully in her sleep," I tell him.

"Ah. And do you know when ... have you decided on...?"

"The funeral arrangements haven't been made yet."

"Quite so, quite so. Is there anything I can do?"

"No. I don't think so. Thank you for calling."

There really is nothing I can think a butcher might do in the circumstances. Besides, I'm quite sure his offer of help is little more than a formality, well meaning but nevertheless an empty gesture, something you must say to the bereft; there are probably many more such calls to come, I realise.

And so it turns out. There are more calls quite soon. Most of the early callers are men, among them some I know, including J.P. Cannock from the Jobcentre and college lecturer and a former student contemporary of mum's, Ryan Makim (that's a name I had heard quite recently too). Some, though, are complete strangers, and I start wondering if I should be taking their names down, and at least their telephone numbers, so that I can eventually ask them to the funeral. But most are happy to just say their piece, briefly. And offer to help – they all did that.

In the middle of one such call there is a ring at the door, and when I say a hasty goodbye and go to open it a delivery girl appears behind a bunch of flowers. Like the phone calls, there are many more of these to come, including bouquets left on the doorstep without a knock. All bear small cards proffering sympathy and commiseration. I take them in, putting them on the sofa for want of a better idea of what to do with them. After a bit

I start to think they might all perish from lack of water. I gather them up and stand them, still in their wrappers, in the bath, running-in some cold water.

While I am doing this the bell rings again. This time I find Carol with yet more flowers. She is in her best clothes, teetering on impossibly high stilettos. Baby Toby is parked just inside the gate behind her.

Chapter 13 A family man?

She steps forward and kisses me on the cheek: despite the posh get-up she still smells of warm milk.

"Hiya. You all right?"

She thrusts the flowers at me.

"These are for you. For your mum. I heard."

"Thanks."

I feel genuinely grateful ... it is a nice gesture and I know she isn't acting on anyone else's behalf, unlike the permanently-smiling florists' assistants. I think I should ask her in but she is already turning.

"I gotta go. Toby's clinic. Let me know when..."

Is everyone going to talk to me now without finishing their questions?

"I'll tell you when I know," I say after her.

"Seeya."

And she click-clacks away, pushchair wheels rattling over the broken paving slabs, turning once to give a little wave before I go back in. I take her flowers to the bathroom to put them with the earlier arrivals.

***

The vicar calls quite late. I have never talked to him before, ever, and don't even know his name. He has a pleasant face, round and a bit red with close-cut greying hair that might have been curly had it been longer. He wears a neat salt-and-pepper tweed suit with a black shirt.

"I'm Clive," he says, not venturing a title or a surname. I do not even know his denomination, though I assume he is Church of England. "I'm sorry I'm so late, Peter – services and things, you know. I would have come sooner if I could. Sorry to hear about Mum."

We stay on the doorstep. I'm not sure if it's a passing call. His next sentence is a bit of a surprise.

"I knew her quite well, actually."

Inward jolt. Another man who would have been about the right age? Another potential dad? I am by now beginning to think anything might be possible, anything at all, including this man in a dog-collar.

"Yes," I agree, shuffling awkwardly on the doorstep. "It is all a bit of a shock."

He does not turn and go. I do not know what else to say. There is a lengthy embarrassed silence.

"Er, could I come in?" he suggests. "There may be quite a bit to talk about."

I show him in, though I cannot imagine what he intends to talk about.

"Do you want some tea?"

By now it is clear that the principal duty in any bereavement is making tea, pot after pot, cup after cup.

"That would be nice. Very kind. Thank you."

He sits upright on the settee, a stiff pose which he still holds when I bring things back from the kitchen. He is not to know her body so recently lay there.

"Cheers," he says, raising his mug to me. It strikes me as an odd thing to say under the circumstances, but I raise my mug nevertheless.

"Now, business. Do you know if Mum wanted a burial or a cremation? Or do you feel is it too early to talk about that?"

"It's fine. I'm all right. But I don't know what she wanted, really I don't."

"And what about a service?"

"I don't know. The Social Services man said we could have a service at the crematorium."

Clive laughs, a slightly false laugh, I feel, and says, "Yes, well, they're all very humanist round at the council, not to say alternative. You haven't agreed to anything yet?"

"No."

"Good. Then can I suggest a service either at Jimmy's or the crematorium, Christian of course, and as we have a newly consecrated burial ground extension, I'd be happy to lay Mum to rest there. Or we can bury her ashes there, if that's what you wish. Keeps it in the parish, you see, among friends. Continuity. Just a suggestion, of course. Think about it. Whatever you want the undertakers will cooperate fully. Who are you with – the Co-op?"

He comes from the 19th century red brick Anglican church two blocks away, then, St James', widely known as Jimmy's.

"When do we have to decide all that?"

"Sooner the better really. Tomorrow is fine ... I wouldn't leave it too long, though. Then you put a notice in the paper. And do write to any friends of hers you can think of. And perhaps you would like to think of a small reception afterwards, tea and sandwiches, beer maybe, at home or in a pub, for friends. Here, take this..."

He produces a card.

"You said you knew Mum?"

"We were around at the same time. I went on to college with a mutual friend, Ryan Makim. I went on to theological college and he went into teaching. And now we've both ended up back here. Amazing, isn't it?"

I nod, even though I can't really see what makes it so amazing. Perhaps I am missing something. Shortly after that Clive the vicar leaves.

I get one last late call. It is from Roy Selincourt's mum. She wants to know if I was with her son last night. Roy's mum is a bit deaf, and you always have to shout to make her hear, especially on the phone.

"No. Why?"

"He's in hospital. He's sick, quite bad."

Oh dear. If somebody from Roy's family says he's sick you can be sure it's more than just a mere broken limb.

"What's the matter with him? What happened?"

"Oh, in trouble again, that's all. It's drink does it," she says. "How's your Mum, by the way?"

She does not know. There must be others who don't yet know, in spite of the efficient town grapevine.

"I'm sorry to have to tell you she's dead Mrs Selincourt. She died last night."

There is a pause. Then she says "Oh", and a few blinks later, "Oh dear." And she puts the phone down leaving me listening to the dialling tone.

I sit in my chair in silence for a long, long while after that. It is just like it used to be, sitting with Mum there, on the settee. Only she isn't there anymore...

I wake suddenly with my chin on my chest, stiff. I must have nodded off, out for hours. Weary beyond words, I drag myself upstairs to bed and fall into it, still in the clothes I had put on so happily that morning. The tears flood back.

***

The next morning, I wake late and experience brief blissful moments before my problems catch up with me.

At 11 o'clock-ish a small, neat, rather sweet man, who introduces himself as Michael Petal from the Co-op Funeral Service, is my first caller. I am in a bit of a dither when I answer the door. I have gone through all the business of preparing myself for the day, washing and putting on fresh clothes, and since all this has taken place upstairs it has been easier to avoid constantly thinking about Mum. Once downstairs, however, faced with the empty sofa, I do not have a clue what to do next. Which is when my visitor knocks at the door. In the death industry at least, things seem to run efficiently 24-7.

Petal has been talking with the vicar, he says in a quiet, calm voice, to secure the church and a burial plot, and everything is fixed for 1pm on Friday so long as I agree.

I agree. I do not know of any better alternative. A trip to the Westcountry with a jar of ashes had seemed to me a difficult thing to plan even if I could think so very far ahead. I wouldn't know where to start, not knowing properly how to get back to that very spot where we were once happy. It was in a land of jumbled memories.

I tell Petal I am grateful for the burial arrangements made on my behalf, and I see a smooth business operation at work underneath all his planning.

"I must give you a quote of course," he says. "You need to know what costs you are facing and there are of course alternatives, although the Co-op is really competitive on price. You can trust me on that. We have to go through the formalities and make it clear everything is entirely your choice, as next of kin. The powers that be do make rather a meal out of all this. That's why we're here to help."

He produces papers to sign, forms to be filled. There is a rigmarole to go through to record the death, he explains, and he tells me how to go about it and obtain the necessary certificate. Finally, he tells me the sort of details people put in the paper about funerals and says he can look after this too if I wish. Again, I agree. Looking pleased he takes a little notebook from his pocket and starts to write things down.

"Good. And have we thought about the service?"

We...I have not, of course. I did not even know when it was being held until I was presented with the arrangements.

"Any favourite hymns, for example?" he prompts. "Or music? And would anyone like to speak? Perhaps not you, of course, that would be understandable. And we like to think of celebrating someone's life rather than being unremittingly sad. Does that sound like the way we should go?"

I am being hurried along too fast for my thoughts.

"Would you like the vicar to arrange things perhaps?" he ventures when I stay silent, trying to get my mind round it all. "I'm quite sure he would be happy to do so. And do you perhaps know how many people might attend?"

"She liked *Onward Christian Soldiers*," I say, at last finding my tongue. If I left it all to him even the music choices would without doubt be made on my behalf.

"And she loved *Morning has Broken* – the one Cat Stevens sings, you know. And she likes ... she liked Joni Mitchell. She played all the new Joni Mitchells whenever they came out."

This is duly noted down. I do not know how many people will come, I tell him, and nor did I know whether I would be able to speak or find that too much of an ordeal. And I ask him what the vicar might say at the service.

"Well, he will call on you on Thursday night, I would think, and ask a few things about your mother, little personal details he needs to know. And he will work out an order of service with us. But if you use any discs or records, we will have to have them before the service. Now, what about afterwards?"

"Afterwards? Afterwards I don't know what I'll do."

I can't think beyond a few hours, minutes come to that.

"A pub perhaps? Or would you like to hold a small gathering here at home?"

I realise suddenly he isn't talking about my future. That's of no concern at all to him.

"There's the Stuton Arms across the road from the church ... they're used to catering for these occasions, and quite cheap ... a couple of pounds a head, that's all. Perhaps better than at home. You don't really want all the business of clearing up, do you?"

"No."

"Shall I call the pub and make the arrangements?"

"Do people have to pay for themselves?"

He smiles. "Not usually. Shall we look at the total costs you are going to face? You don't need to worry about any of it until a couple of weeks afterwards, when we send you the bill ... but I gather mum's left money to cover it all? And there may be grants, that sort of thing, you can take advantage of. We'll help you look into all that."

He bends over his notebook and scribbles some figures, ending with a flourish then turning his notebook around so that I can read.

"Something in the region of this..."

It seems quite a large sum to me, but I have read newspaper articles about the high costs of dying. I tell him I agree. What else can I do? We shake hands.

***

Shortly after that, Dr Cohen calls by again.

"Just popped in to see if everything's all right."

I tell him the arrangements I have just made with Petal.

"Good," he says. "And how are you feeling now? Coping? Eating, I hope."

"I'm fine."

I feel I am for the moment.

"You know, grief can be a very long process of adjusting to loss at least, perhaps even years, especially in a close lifelong relationship like yours," he says. "Don't be afraid to ask for help. The clinic can put you in touch with a counsellor."

"Thanks."

"Not drinking too much, are you?"

He means alcohol. I haven't even thought about it.

"No. Not at all."

"Good lad."

He pats me on the shoulder and leaves, after which I cry all the while I am frying myself bacon and eggs and a piece of stale bread, still operating awkwardly with my glued-up hand and its nestling coin. Something, I realise, will have to be done about that. But not at Dr Cohen's surgery. I am too embarrassed about it for that, and anyway the clinic is not open until Monday morning, tomorrow. That's when I remember the hospital and Roy Selincourt.

***

I am still not hungry even though I yesterday ate nothing but biscuits washed down with cup after cup of tea. After I have made myself eat some of the fry-up, I leave the house for what seems like the first time in quite a while and head for A&E to see what they can do about my hand.

It is raining lightly. My legs feel a bit funny, but it is surprisingly good to be in the open air and look at the sky, even if it is now full of scudding grey clouds.

Our hospital is a massive pile of pebbledashed 60s concrete which the town is forever dreaming of replacing with something modelled on the slick operations depicted in the TV soaps.

It has a run-down air with paint peeling here and there, and broken floor tiles and ancient-looking plumbing. But all the staff seem to manage to ignore this and move around with an air of

169

cheerful optimism. Maybe they are helping themselves to the medicine cabinet. I'm directed to a cubicle.

"Jesus, not another one. Put your hand on here and keep it still."

A cross-looking young woman intern in a white overall, a redhead, pushes my hand firmly down on a stainless-steel table with one hand, violently shaking a bottle of solvent spray with the other. I don't know if it is her red hair that reminds me of my recent encounter or the sensation of being manhandled, but there is a definite stirring in my libido. I try to stop thinking about it.

"What have you all been up to?" she carries on, squirting a liberal amount of the yellowy liquid all over my hand and down between the fingers. "We had four yesterday ... now you. As if the bloody boozers last night weren't enough."

My seized-up fist foams and stings.

"I was modelling," I say lamely. "Model aeroplanes, I mean. Just made a mistake. I didn't know it would stick like this."

"Mmm."

We're interrupted by a ghastly groan from a curtained cubicle somewhere close. From further away, I can hear pained, rhythmic, unending shouts: *Nurse, Nurse, nurse...*"

She ignores all this and examines my fist from all angles then lets it drop. "Wait here a few moments and I'll be back," she says, and pushes her way out through the curtains.

The medical staff are clearly busy. All the cubicles seem full and apparently, she is the only skilled person on duty to look after them. Behind me, I know, the waiting room is crowded.

170

I try to flex my hand. There is more movement than was possible minutes ago. By the time she reappears I have a couple of fingers free, but not the coin. I have also helped myself to more spray, hoping to speed the process.

"Oh," she says sarcastically, "Self-medication, eh? Pardon me for interrupting."

Tutting, she prizes the last of my fingers apart and jiggles the coin until it unsticks from my palm.

"When *I* was a little boy, we used to make planes with balsa wood and glue you could get high on," she observed drily. "Superglue is a bit of a step up from that. I don't suppose any of you are going to tell me why you are all stuck to 5p pieces?"

She gives me a tissue to clean up the last of the goo and rubs the coin clean on another one.

"Here," she says, smiling and flipping it through the air at me, "Keep your measly tip." And with that she is gone.

I ask at reception where I might find Roy. They want to know what he is in for, but I don't really know. In the end they trace him to Ward 4B, which is on the fourth floor. I ask when it is visiting time and they laugh and say nobody bothers with that anymore and people can just walk in and out whenever they want, which doesn't say much for security.

I must ride up in a shuddering lift big enough to take several hospital trolleys and with doors on two sides for people to go in and out, which is all very confusing when you come to the place you want but don't know which side it is best to get out.

I eventually find Roy in a biggish ward propped up in bed reading a magazine and looking, for him anyway, a picture of health.

"Hello. Have a grape," he says, pointing to the bowl of fruit on the bedside cabinet. "They're really nice. Sables."

"What's wrong?" I ask, cautious.

"Exposure," he says with a touch of indignation. "And fatigue. Extreme fatigue. And possible pneumonia. Only got stuck up on the railings by those little bastards in the park, that's all. With superglue."

So, Roy was the crucifixion victim who Goldilocks and I sped past in the night, abandoning him to his fate. Poor, lame, easygoing Roy, who never hurt a fly in his life. They'd found him easy meat, my asylum-seeking friends. They were more than likely in cahoots with the little angel who stuck me up with the coin. They'd escorted poor Roy, limping, to the railings by the bowling green, and then made him stand on a wooden box while they plastered his hands with superglue and got him to spread his arms wide and hang onto the iron crossbar at either side. After waiting for the glue to set and committing the final degradation of dropping his trousers and pants to his ankles, they had kicked the box away and had run off cackling into the dark while all the hullabaloo by the lake blew up. I dared not say anything about me and Goldilocks passing by in the night.

"Christ," I say. "Good job it wasn't very cold."

"It was bloody cold enough. And they had to bring me in with bits of railing struck to my hands after the fire brigade cut me out. Still, I'm not as bad as *him*."

He nods towards the next bed. I haven't really noticed before but now I see there is a shapeless figure in pyjamas, his back to us.

"And what happened to him? Who is it?"

172

"Ballard."

I'm aghast.

"Hell, what happened to him?"

"He got impaled on one of the spikes, poor bastard."

"Ballard? Really? How? Where?"

Roy smirks.

"Up his bum," he says with relish.

To my horror, the figure I had thought to be asleep gives a groan and turns over to regard us. He has clearly been awake for some time.

A bloodshot, pained eye opens, looks first at me then Roy.

"Don't you tell anyone one word of this, Walker or Selincourt, you hear?"

Ballard is trying to sound menacing, but he should know the effect is not altogether impressive when you are lying in bed in pyjamas. I just stare.

"Just don't!"

And he rolls back over and looks away.

Without paying heed to Ballard's threats, Roy tells me that after his own crucifixion a whole lot of people had streamed over the railings without stopping, despite his desperate pleas for somebody, anybody, to stop and help. I wince again. Ballard, to his misfortune, had had the misfortune to slip while going over the top, his agility obviously not in the same league as that of the twenty-somethings he kept company with. Roy said Ballard spent most of the time bleating about all his blood draining away. Detained side by side, suspended above the bowling green, they had kept one another company of sorts through most of the night until discovered by a fisherman making his way to the lake at first light.

Roy falls silent. Now it is my turn.

"My Mum died Friday night."

He turns away as if looking at something on the other side of his bed.

"Oh," he says, using the same words and the same deadpan tone as his mother. "Oh dear."

***

And that was that from Roy. Like mother like son, I think. Is that all it's worth, the end of my Mum? Just 'Oh dear'?

But Ballard suddenly rolls himself back over to look at me. There's astonishment on his face.

"Say that again."

"Mum died Friday night. I found her yesterday morning."

Ballard abruptly rolls his legs out of bed, sits up. A passing nurse frowns but he ignores her. He is genuinely shocked.

"No! Not really?"

"I'm afraid so."

"Christ, I can't believe it."

"Neither can I, properly."

He looks away and then back again with sympathy in his eyes. There are tears too.

"God, I'm sorry Pete. Really sorry. You must feel awful."

"It's a shock. It's pretty hard to take."

He looks away again, shaking his head. "It would be," he says. "It is. Did she...?"

I am ready with the responses now. "She died peacefully, in her sleep."

"Have you...?"

"The funeral's on Friday, one o'clock at St James'."

"Oh hell." He stands up carefully. "I've got to get out of here."

I leave Ballard dressing himself painfully, glaring at a reproving nurse. Roy has still not said any more, nor has he even looked at me.

***

It is remarkable that you can sometimes walk around this town and not meet anyone you know, but I do that for a lot of Sunday afternoon after leaving the luckless pair in hospital.

Eventually I find myself going to the bowling green to witness the gap in the railings where the crucified Roy has been sawn free. The wooden orange crate on which he had presumably been perched is still there, kicked under a laurel bush. I can't see any of Ballard's blood, though I try to find some sign of his demise. By the lake, there is a scorched patch from the bonfire but everything else has been tidied up. I spend some time by the lake, just sitting (although the benches are wet) and looking at the water and the water birds and the rising fish.

I cry again. I find I can now do so silently. If anyone comes along they will not really know how I feel. But nobody comes along.

After a while I feel very hungry and get up, turn towards home. Despite the hunger my feet drag. It is difficult to put the key in the lock, turn it, open the door.

The house is cold, empty. It feels abandoned. I turn on the gas fire and the television, loud, to fill the emptiness with warmth and noise.

That evening I cook myself two suppers, the first of fish fingers with mash and the other, since I am still starving, two fried eggs and some oven chips. I eat while watching television, which I leave on whatever is showing, not taking in a great deal. I also drink lots of flat Coke – you know, those big bottles you always have in the fridge, God knows how old – and many more cups of tea. So long as I am eating or drinking, I can cope, everything feels sort of all right. If I stop for any length of time, I find myself crying again. A thirst for alcohol comes suddenly and I remember there is a bottle of sherry on top of the fridge, a hangover from Christmas. But somehow it does not appeal enough for me to go and fetch it.

By nine o'clock I am exhausted and bloated and go to bed. Getting through the day has been quite an achievement.

***

On Monday morning it is raining again. I get up and dress and once more I'm nonplussed in the sitting room about what to do first until it crosses my mind I needed to buy a paper to see if the notice about Mum's death has been published. I am halfway to Singh's when I remember the first edition of the *Argus*, unless it's a special like the match report, is not printed until around 11am and often does not reach Singh's emporium until noon. It is not yet nine o'clock. I carry on, straight past the paper shop and on into town, this time skirting the park.

Town looks different, feels different. People are scurrying everywhere, preoccupied with getting to work, and after a while

176

I kid myself I am part of this whole morning activity, so much so that I begin to hurry along myself, though I have nothing urgent to do, no appointments to attend. Hurrying with me are people in suits, uniforms, overalls, all desperate to get to their jobs. Once there, they can sell one another food, insurance, books, cut glass decanters, handbags, shoes and cars, and then there will be a little gap in all this activity for lunch followed by another frantic trading period up to the early evening. Then they will all go home, change clothes and go out to meet one another, call on one another, as if they haven't been crazily taking away each other's money all day long.

But after nine o'clock it falls quiet on the roads and pavements, and I can slow down, start to go from shop window to shop window, studying the contents, most of which I really do not see, as I make my way along the old High Street, which is still practically the only real shopping street in town if you do not count the new mall on the outskirts. What people there are about now are in ones and twos, elderly people, those who did not have jobs I guess. I see none of them go into shops: in fact, they are all behaving rather like me. A little later, some younger women start to appear, some with pushchairs, the young mums I suppose, and some of them do enter shops and emerge with carrier bags. When I run out of shops on one side of the road I turn and go back on the other side until I am near my start point again. I am about to turn again to go back over my tracks when I see I am outside the Co-op Funeral Service office. In a window full of polished marble urns and neatly engraved gravestones is some elaborate gilt lettering on a wooden screen. It reads 'Chapel of Rest'.

Mum is in there I know. Without thinking I have my hand on the door handle, ready to enter, when I stop. What if they have done things to her, made up her face, that sort of thing? If I go in and find they have taken away her smile I don't think I will be able to bear it. I step back, eyes watering again, and move on, hoping nobody has recognised me from within, dreading someone will spring out and call me back.

A pub sign catches my attention, illuminated by a sudden shaft of sunlight as the filmy clouds above begin to break up, heralding a sunny afternoon. It is one of those small pubs between shops you normally don't notice because it is so familiar yet anonymous, a pub you suspect of being dingy within, the brown cut glass window panes being impenetrable, and full of pensioners playing cribbage and drinking dark mild ale. The Prince Albert, says the sign with its nondescript face distinguished only by a slicked down coif and a high wing collar. I don't think I've ever noticed the sign before, consciously anyway.

A sudden silence falls over everything inside, hubbub dying as I enter the small room with its one corner bar. I swear even the cigarette smoke coils hanging in the filtered sunbeams stop moving at my entrance. I order a pint of bitter at the bar from a short and taciturn man with black oiled hair and a moustache, waistcoated. The order is seen to in silence, the cash transaction too.

There was indeed a game, dominoes perhaps, under way at one of the brown-topped tables. It had been in full swing before my obvious intrusion halted things.

There are few tables and all of them are occupied, mostly by men and women with full plastic shopping bags gathered about their feet. The atmosphere reeks of stale beer and nicotine. There is nowhere to sit let alone hide in a corner which is what I really want to do. So I stand at the bar and only manage to get a bit more than half the drink finished before I feel so self conscious I must go.

"Thanks," I murmur, and make my way back out gratefully into a sunlit day all the brighter because of the dinginess and silent, unwarranted hostility I have just left behind.

But I also find something fundamental inside me has changed, maybe because I have not long ago turned away from the undertakers. I have a new lightness which can hardly be attributed to the small amount of beer I have just downed. Maybe it is because the finality of it all has just hit me. Now I realise it is time to start thinking about adjusting and perhaps moving on. Life is continuing, and if I am not careful it will pass me by, leave me in a netherworld like it left the inhabitants of the Prince Albert.

A paper seller, an ancient everyone calls Cyril in a greasy gabardine mac (worn summer and winter alike), is calling outside the big open loading bay below the *Argus* building just a little way down the street. Vans bearing the paper's yellow and black livery are starting to stream out. The first edition is rolling and there is a dull rumble from the presses within. It is impossible to decipher Cyril's grunted enticements to buy his papers, but when I pay for a copy, the front-page story catches my eye before I can turn inside to look at the death notices.

The headline, in a type size papers usually hold in reserve for the Second Coming, reads *PARK MAYHEM* and beneath it in lesser sizes are headlines proclaiming *RIOT ACT READ*, and *Our man injured in serious fracas*. That would be Ballard then.

The story is lurid but not all that far from the truth, except for a statement on the numbers of people involved which are a little on the high side for veracity. Inside stories say there have been several arrests and civic leaders are calling for action to stop '*this sort of unacceptable behaviour*'. However, nobody has cared to speculate how rare such occasions are and when one might be likely to happen again. Despite that there is plenty of indignation in the air.

The fact that none of those arrested has been detained or charged with any offence appears well down the main story, where it will not interfere with the dramatic headlines. Reading between the lines I feel sure the police enjoyed the occasion as much as my fellow revellers.

The only truly unhappy people were the wake-goers like me who had run foul of the glue gang, such as the luckless Ballard, and the civic leaders who hadn't been involved in the best lark the town has witnessed since the celebrations at the end of the Second World War.

All of this I digest at a slow stroll. Then I flip a few pages until I came to Births, Marriages and Deaths and run my eye up and down the columns until it jumps out: *WALKER - MARY JANE*. I stop to read it. It is all there, the details of the funeral, where and when, and would people who wished please send flowers to the Co-op funeral parlour, the place I almost just visited.

That notice ought to do it, I think. Anyone in this town will either read it or someone will tell them they have seen it, and where. But then the sudden thought grabs me that there might be other people important to Mum but who did not live in our town anymore. I now know, you see, that she, Ballard, Roger

Stenton, everyone inhabits a small world which has this town as its focal point. Some might have escaped, but there is precious little significant contact with the wide world outside. The escapees she has known, if indeed there are any, could well be entries in her address book. I quicken my step and head home with the resolve of writing to whoever else might need to know about the funeral.

I am almost past the newsagents when I remembered I have no stamps if I want to send out letters. I stop and go in. At the counter as usual is Mr Singh.

"I'm deeply sorry, so sorry to hear," he says, bowing his head as I approach. "I will stop saving the magazines until you decide what to do."

He smiles, a kindly lined face under his turban. I thank him and buy two books of first-class stamps and then, as an afterthought, select a packet of Basildon Bond envelopes and a writing pad of the same make from the stationery rack to the side of the counter. Somewhere behind him there is movement and I focus to see one of his girls in the storeroom. She does not look my way. Everyone here knows, then. Anyway, nothing can harm me anymore. I no longer have to fear the tit-juggler or feel I must put her in her place.

As I set out again for home, I am surprised how brisk and business-like I am feeling. It even crosses my mind that I have this grief thing under control. I mean, never mind the two years or more of grief prescribed by Dr Cohen. The fact is I have been grieving for Mum for as long as she has been ill, watching her turning to a withered dry stick of pain before my eyes, this lovely woman who has guarded me all my life, watched me grow, held my hand on the way to school, scrimped to see me

181

fed and clothed and given an education, however worthless it seems.

I have been grieving as her mobility left her, grieving sometimes as if she was already dead. All that hope her various medical attendants have taken pains to impress on me has been exposed as false. They well knew the outcome all along, didn't they?

I reach home. More flowers are piled in the doorway, more envelopes lie on the doormat. I go inside, hang my jacket in the hall, go into the sitting room and see the flowers already on the sofa. And again I weep, suddenly and silently, tears streaming down my face, my purchases falling out of my hand.

***

It is some time before I pull myself together and go to the kitchen. I pour myself a glass of milk because I cannot be bothered to make any tea.

I find the address book again and go through it. But there are very few entries, and none for the likes of Ballard and Roger Stenton. Because of the closeness of the people in this town, I realise, it hasn't been necessary for her to make notes of how to find anyone. Most addresses were well known to her, and if anyone disappeared somebody would tell her where they had gone, who with and why.

In the end I write to no-one. The few out-of-town entries look incredibly old and faded and the names mean nothing to me. Mum has never mentioned them. I put the book away again, place the unopened packet of stamps and writing material on the sideboard.

I make myself food, more from the need to occupy myself rather than from hunger. In the process I see the sherry bottle on top of the fridge and take it down. It is still a good two thirds full. I take it to the sink where I rinse a dirty glass, uncork the bottle and pour. A sharp smell hits my nostrils. The sherry has turned to vinegar. I cork it up again and put it back.

I eat mechanically, watching the television news. The Japanese football debacle and its aftermath have quickly fallen out of newsworthiness. I go to bed early although it is still only the afternoon, because there is nothing, really nothing, that I can think of to do.

***

That night, and in the intervening nights before the funeral, I find myself sleeping surprisingly soundly, especially after spells of deep misery. I know I am intensely lonely. In the house flowers, and cards especially, mount up daily. The bath is full of them and therefore I can only splash-wash myself in the washbasin. There is almost nowhere to sit in the sitting room for the bunches and bouquets on all the seats and nowhere at all to stand up the steady stream of cards, so I continue making them into flat stacks on the sideboard. I rarely stay any time in the room, just using it as a transit station between upstairs and the the kitchen or the front door. I had no idea quite so many people knew Mum.

They are strange days. Tuesday is usually a useless day to my mind when very little happens and there is never anything in the post except credit card and car insurance junk mail. This Tuesday, though, it takes all the morning and a bit of the afternoon to come away from the local registry office with the three copies of Mum's death certificate they suggest I might need. I am glad of such time-wasting, however, and quite grateful when the other business of the day, starting moves to close Mum's savings account and bank account, prove to be just as long-winded to sort out.

Wednesday drives me to drink: unable to stay in the house I again visit the High Street and once again, after pausing at the door of the funeral parlour and lacking nerve to enter, I gingerly go into the Prince Albert.

It is as if nothing had changed. All the faces, even the coils of grey-blue smoke, are the same as when I last walked out. I order a pint, and again I cannot finish it before feeling I should leave. But the sips I do take start something, and out in the fresh air again I decide I have a definite need for alcohol. I cannot face the Tap, however, for fear I will run into someone I know. In the end I go to a chain off-licence, a few doors from the Prince Albert and on the way home. I buy a litre of whisky, going for the cheapest I can find. The purchase virtually cleans me out of cash. Back at home more flowers and cards are waiting.

The liquor is rough. I sip at the first drink, about a third of a tumbler (I bought no mixers). The second drink of a similar size goes down quite well. I am halfway down the third when the phone rings. It is Carol: Am I alone? Would it be all right if she comes round? She will have to bring Toby, but he will sleep. She won't stay long. Just for a chat?

I put her off. Lonely though I am I cannot bear to think of being in someone's company. Embarrassingly, too, I am starting to slur my words. Putting the phone down, I stumble bit getting up and spill what is left of the drink down my trousers. Looking at the soaking leg I realise I have nothing to wear for the funeral. A sort of deep woe settles on me and there is nothing for it but to go to bed again, though it isn't all that late. I cap the bottle and put it beside the sherry vinegar on the fridge before heading to my refuge upstairs.

***

On Thursday, the clothes problem is the first thing that comes to mind when I wake. First, however, I must make my regular call at the Jobcentre. When the dreadful Joker calls out my name, however, Cannock immediately emerges from his eyrie behind him and says to the minion: "Ask Mr Walker to pop behind the counter and see me will you, Mr Jones?"

Scowling, Jones disappears from his booth and reappears at a side door, ushers me into the inner sanctum. I walk behind him to Cannock's office. Joker's neck seems to have a crick, for he keeps twisting it in a peculiar way. Or perhaps he has developed a tic. He pulls Cannock's door open for me to enter, taking care not to meet my eyes.

J.P. Cannock rises to meet me, holding out a hand. Jones slopes away.

"Come in and shut the door. And sit down, Peter, please."

We shake hands. He's using my first name. Why? What is this? Surely the relaxed attitudes of the 21st century have not suddenly managed to penetrate the local Jobcentre, a starchy institution if ever there is one where people still wear ties and you get the impression they would rather not have any clients to bother them, especially the younger ones.

"I am deeply sorry to hear about your mother. Very sorry indeed."

He sits, shaking his head sadly and looking down at the desktop. He does seem sorry. Then he picks up a biro and holds

185

each end of it, arms flat on the surface, to give his hands something to do I expect.

"I have been reviewing your case," he says, bringing up his milky eyes to meet mine. "You don't seem to have had much of a fair chance, it seems to me. A fault of the poor range of employment opportunities in this town more than anything, I fear, because you seem quite willing, and you do have a college degree."

"It has been hard to find anything suitable," I offer.

"Mmm. Have you ever thought of the Civil Service?" He lifts the pen with one hand and sweeps it round in the air to indicate all that surrounds us. "It is not a bad bet. And it is full of opportunities. Plus there are many benefits."

Is he offering me a job? Here? Now? I feel my eyes widening. He continues.

"It so happens that I have a vacancy here. Two as a matter of fact, but one will be an internal promotion. I am prepared to recommend you for the post. In fact, I think you would be an asset. But do please take time to think about it. You must have a lot on your plate. A lot."

He *is* offering me a job!

"Will that be on the counter?" I ask, knowing this to be the starting place of Joker Jones, presumably the first rung on the Civil Service ladder.

"No. You'll start as a temporary officer of course which is where everyone starts but this is slightly higher up the scale and behind the scenes. And it leads on to team leadership and office management, once I get some idea of your calibre."

Does this mean I could be a notch above Joker? How sweet that would be. I am nearly carried away with this thought before I remember the scorn and pity with which I regard Jobcentre staff to this point. Yes, even Cannock I'm afraid. It is the pits, from its dull battleship grey walls and screwed down seats to its probably terminally boring routine tasks. If Cannock does not outwardly display cobwebs, there must be some in his head.

"Thank you," I say lamely, not quite knowing how to reply. "When would you like to know?"

There are many more questions I should ask, I know, like working conditions, pay and suchlike, but I am taken aback by the offer. I start rising to leave but Cannock waves me down again. He coughs to clear his throat.

"By the way, on a rather different subject..."

He is now looking over my left shoulder.

"I gather you know, er, Glynnis, my daughter?"

I start to blush. It doesn't take much to turn me crimson.

"N...no," I fluster, "I mean, yes... I mean we met briefly, but that's all. I know her."

"But not what you would call a relationship?" says Cannock, this time fastening his eyes on mine. They reveal fatherly anxiety. He places considerable weight on the word 'relationship'.

"N...no."

I do not dare to say otherwise. Fortunately, it appears to be the right thing to say. There's something akin to relief on his face.

"I see."

His watery eyes drop again.

"She's going through a very difficult period. Difficult. Wants to leave town although it's not a good idea at her age. There have been boyfriends ... none of them a great success. I'm rather glad she has you as a friend, however, and I'm glad it's not anything ... well, deeper. That might be difficult."

What the fuck does he mean by that?

He looks up again.

"On an even more personal level I will attend your mother's ceremony tomorrow," he says. "Now, do have a think about that post with us. I'm sure you will see it makes sense, though I don't want you to feel in any way pressurised. We will talk further about it next week if you like. It's not very urgent. And today's paperwork has all been seen to. There's no need to go through all that rigmarole this week, though of course there will be changes to your circumstances which we will need to discuss in time."

He stands up while he's saying this, the interview over. We shake hands and I leave. As I cross the waiting room I feel Joker's eyes boring into my back, and I know he would love to know exactly what was going on in there.

But what has it all been about? Is Cannock warning me off Glynnis? The more I think about it the more it seems so. But a job offer. That seems to be trying to push me in another direction, make me more acceptable as a possible suitor for Glynnis perhaps? It is all very confusing. Should I do it? Could I do it, more to the point? With Jones working in the same office, is it a wise move?

But for the moment I have more pressing problems. Lack of suitable wear for a funeral for a start. That means money, and I realise I should have made a plea for emergency funds from the Jobcentre. Too late now. It crosses my mind that perhaps the bank, or rather Mum's building society, can help. A couple of days ago in the building society office things were being transferred to my name, and at that time the finality of it all upset me and made it hard to think of going back to ask for cash.

However, I do, and this time things have changed. The woman at the reception counter calls details up on a screen and directs me to a girl seated at a desk. She is expecting me when I sit down and I ask if I might have some money immediately, not entirely confident it will be at all easy. Yes, Mr Walker, she says with a wide smile, of course it is possible to release some of the money. Would £1,000 be all right for the time being? It might take a few more days to clear the rest. I almost fall over. These are riches beyond my imaginings. Trying to keep my head and behave like someone who regularly handles such sums of money, I ask for £500. She writes a voucher without a blink and directs me back to the cash counter where a clerk counts it out in £20s and hands it over. Shocked, I do not even get out my wallet but cram the notes into my pocket, muttering my thanks, and leave in something of a dream. For the very first time in my life, I am carrying £500 in hard cash!

Does it turn me instantly into a spendthrift? It crosses my mind that I could have a whale of a time with such a sum, a Majorca holiday for example. It's the first relief from dour thoughts I have had for some time. But it turns out that I have become more frugal than I have ever been. I shop very carefully indeed for the sort of clothes I think will be appropriate for tomorrow – a dark jacket and trousers, a white shirt, black shoes.

The money also turns me into ... well, into an anxious somebody carrying a large amount of cash around. In short, a vulnerable mark for every snatch thief or thug in town. I am very glad indeed when I arrive home with my purchases and the rest of the cash, and finally shut the door behind me.

But the peace does not last long. I have just laid out my new clothes on my bed when the doorbell rings. I have a date with the vicar, I remember. I carefully hang up the clothes before going down to answer the door.

And it is him, Clive. I ask him in and clear a space for him on the settee among the latest flowers and make some tea while he waits fiddling with a pen, a notebook open on his lap.

"Now," he says when we are both sitting down. "Tell me all about Mum. Some of it I know, of course, but it's little things people like to remember. The things she liked, people she admired and aspired to. And the ordinary facts of course, her school days, that sort of thing."

And so I tell him about the ordinary things. She went to the grammar school, as it then was – the school which later became the comprehensive I attended. She'd been an only child, her own father, a solicitor's clerk and later a regimental sergeant major with aspirations of being a writer, dying while she was still a child. I had come along late in her life, at 30 or so. Herself, she had never quite known what to do, and instead did many things. She'd been a Woolworths girl, a BHS manageress before her managerial career was cut short by pregnancy, the school dinner lady, and most recently a part-time negotiator for Weston's estate agents. She liked country walks, our occasional holidays by the sea. Her favourite colour was blue, her favourite flowers were roses.

What don't I tell him? That I have lost my best, my only friend, someone who was always there even while I was being cared for by Gran, my surrogate mother in the early days while Mum worked in dire jobs to help us all scrape by. Though I say nothing of it I vividly recall her holding my hand, taking me to school, comforting me whenever I was physically or mentally hurt, encouraging me always ... even up to the end, when I really haven't been making my way in this town.

Something will turn up, Petey, she would always say, don't worry, something will turn up. This was of course delivered with one of her smiles that made you feel good about yourself no matter what.

And I don't tell him she is a murderer, although that fact too comes all too readily back to mind.

When he has gone, I pour myself a big shot of whisky, drink it quickly and make it to bed just as the anaesthetic effect is starting to take hold. At least I have one good friend, that bottle.

Chapter 14 Mum's legacy

We stand at the edge of Mum's grave, a stiff little party with the vicar, who I now know to be the Rev Clive Woodward, having just read his surname for the first time from the board outside the church.

There are about 18 of us all told, and apart from Tania and Carol all are men. I revise my last opinion of Tania, because she cared enough to come after all. Carol has turned out in a smartly cut grey suit with her hair done up, making her look much more grownup than I have ever seen her. There's no Toby this time. She stands beside me, our arms touching. At some point I look up to see Cannock's face opposite. He smiles in much the same way as the elderly couple smiled at me and Carol in the park just a few short days ago. Glynnis is not present.

The day is appropriately wet and windy as we all watch the coffin lowered into the earth. Strangely, I really don't connect this any more with Mum. Clive reads some things about cutting down flowers and we all follow him picking up a bit of soil from the heap beside the hole and letting it fall in on top of the shiny black wooden coffin.

The arrangements earlier in the day worked like clockwork. The funeral car came, and we piled the flowers on Mum's coffin and were whisked to the church, an early elderly man on the street doffing his cap as we passed. It had been a short and quite poignant service. We came in with Joni singing *Big Yellow Taxi*, and all sang *Morning Has Broken*, and Ballard rather touchingly read a Matthew Arnold poem, *Cover Her with Roses*, which was so apt that I felt tears streaming down my face until the last bits about 'vasty halls of death', which is far too gloomy. Glancing up, I saw there were tears all round and even Ballard broke up a bit. It was, after all, supposed to be upbeat. A celebration, Clive insisted, of Mum's life. We go from the church with *I Wish I had a River I could Skate Away On*. She liked that song. I'd like to think of her skating, gliding down an endless river, starlit perhaps, happy and without a care in the world. Yes, that was a good thought.

Now that Mum is in the ground Tania gives me a bosomy hug and leaves the proceedings. The rest of us walk to the pub together, a loose group including the vicar, where a party of 30 has been catered for. Everyone who comes across from the church shakes hands with me. Ballard is almost the last.

Finding ourselves momentarily out of the crush I ask him something that has been on my mind a while.

"Was he there – Derek?"

"Derek?" He frowns.

"Yes ... Derek the aimless drifter, the man you told me about."

He shakes his head as if he does not know what I am talking about. Is he being deliberately obtuse? I am indignant.

"You said about him knowing Mum ... in the Tap, before the party."

"Ohhh," he says, suddenly making the link. "*That* Derek? Look, kid, I'm afraid I made him up. There were hundreds of drifters going through town in those days..."

He is embarrassed, realising what he has just said. He covers up quickly.

"Not all with your mum, of course. I'm sorry, I didn't mean anyone in particular."

I've lost another contender for my father, and I'm crestfallen. Seeing this, Ballard puts an arm round me, hugs.

"See you in the Tap in the week?"

Somebody butts in on this to bore me with some unsurprising reminiscences and shortly afterwards I see Ballard leaving. I reflect that the last witness to his crime, his accomplice, now lies in the ground. I wonder if it makes him sleep any easier. I should think both have revisited the scene in their imaginations many, many times. I know I would have done. It would be like remembering Mike Collins' comments on my painting, only worse. Or finding the graffiti about myself on a toilet wall.

Apart from Cannock there are other men I suspect who know more about Mum than they are letting on, among them Roger Stenton, and the younger and older Mike Westons from the estate agency. Some men at the wake however I do not know. Some of them put themselves in the picture for me, having met Mum at some point in their lives. All are possible father material, I suppose. Nobody reveals themselves as such but none of this matters much any more to me, not under these circumstances anyway.

What does matter, after all, when everything we do, everything we are, comes down to this in the end? What's the point of it all, I ask myself time after time, what's the point? And when Mike Weston jnr asks me if I was thinking about selling the house the same feeling surfaces again. What's the point?

However, I do not say this. Instead, I tell him I have not thought about it, which I haven't, to which he replies that he has lots of customers looking for property like ours where you can walk into town or to the railway station. There has been a big rise in demand since Mum bought it. A wise buy, he calls it.

But what *is* the point?

When the party is over the locals, who have been eyeing us like vultures, tuck into the piles of remaining food with relish.

I am more than a little drunk when I leave the pub and Carol walks home with me. She has not said much all along and now we walk largely in silence. Our fingers are occasionally brushing but not quite connecting. I don't mind this, but I don't know what she is feeling or thinking. I guess she does not know what to say, and neither do I. She kisses me on the cheek at the gate, this time holding my hand briefly and squeezing.

"I won't come in. See you soon?"

"All right," I agree, an empty feeling returning.

I watch her go, then go inside. I'm alone again.

From time to time since Mum died the letters in the keepsakes tin have come into my mind. Once or twice I have held them in my hand, trying to will myself to open them, find out if they are from her lover, a man who might end my quest. Each time I have been unable to untie the ribbon. They have gone back into the tin, with the lid closed over them.

I think of them now.

Before I know it, I am sitting with the bundle of light blue envelopes on my lap, the open tin beside me on the settee. I pull one end of the ribbon and the bow falls open easily, the letters sort of expanding as they are freed as if they are breathing at last. Each is still within its envelope still. I pick up the first, look at the outside. I feel a shock when I notice for the first time the

195

stamps are Israeli. I look at the outsides of several more. All the same, all addressed to Mrs Mary Walker in the same strong clear hand. Gingerly I start to take one out.

A small thing falls out of the folded paper as it comes out of the envelope: a little black and white portrait photograph, signs of wear at the edges. It falls face up. It's a child's face, brown, dark curly hair, eyes that look black, smiling. Confusing possibilities start racing in my head: Did she have another child? Is this her lover's child? What?

I unfold the browning piece of paper, and there's another shock: a formal letterhead, *SOS Children's Charities*.

It's typed.

"Dear Mrs Walker," it starts, "We are pleased once again to update you with the progress of your sponsored Palestinian child Asam Mustafa ..."

What follows is news that Asam was learning well, growing fast and has a promising future in his orphanage camp. I final sentence thanks Mum for her continuing donations and ends with a signature, Fr Michael Stirling ... and I know in an instant what this is all about. And why. I have unearthed Mum's conscience and perhaps her atonement.

I put the letter back in its envelope and read no more. Tying them up clumsily I put them all back in the tin and replace it on the sideboard.

I sit on the sofa, looking round at all the cards, for a long, long time. At least all the flowers have gone. After a while it grows dark but still I sit, without putting the light on. It must be quite late when I go to bed.

Chapter 15 Goodbye to all that

Over a month has passed. I am heading for the the bus station and I'm just about to turn the last corner. I have a smart new bright blue rucksack on my back, new fashionable jeans. New clothes all round in fact. A lot has happened.

I no longer have a home, for a start. Well, I do, but it has been bared down in a drastic clear-out by the local auction rooms and the cash for that now sits in my wallet. No more links with my youth exist anymore. The paintings have gone out with the rubbish, my signatures carefully scoured from any that bore them.

Most important of all, I feel, I have written to Israel to tell Fr Stirling what has happened and to pledge continued support for Asam. Those letters I burned but was unable to throw away the ashes which I carry sealed in another envelope. At some time, I may find an appropriate place for them.

The house was let out practically as soon as it had gone on the market, to a nice young family who want to paint the walls with their own colours. Fine by me. The rent money will go into the bank regularly until I need to sell up. Plenty of time to decide that.

I have not taken up Cannock's offer. In fact, I never went to the Jobcentre again. There were also many excuses I made to to Carol Latham about not being able to meet her and have not actually seen her since the funeral. When I think of it, I let calls from God knows how many people go unanswered.

And I also avoided seeing Ballard. Or rather I avoided him seeing me, for though I once entered the Tap with the express purpose of meeting people, talking with my peers, I found instead that the distant sight of Ballard holding forth to his adoring young court in the hazy bar made me turn about and exit immediately. I went instead to the Prince Albert, a place where the landlady now says "hello" to me and even a few of the denizens nod acknowledgement in my direction.

But that is all behind me now. Where am I going? It doesn't matter, though the first bus I am taking will have London on the destination panel, and I have a week booked in a bed and breakfast between Islington and less fashionable Hackney.

"It doesn't matter what I do" has taken over from "What's the point in doing anything?" It is a progression, however, something beyond, and what is more it allows for myriad possibilities, most distinctly positive rather than negative.

Along with my stripped-down baggage, emotional as well as physical, I still carry a great sadness of course. It is something I could have stayed with in town until it went away, or instead I could choose to get up and go and carry it around with me. Well, I've made my choice.

I turn the corner and see that the bus is in. It picks up passengers in towns far to the west of us before calling in here. And who can I see just getting on but Glynnis Cannock.

She has not seen me. Without knowing why, I pull back, stay out of sight.

I wait until that coach has emerged from the station and swished past me on its way to London before I enter to have my ticket changed. The next bus is only an hour's wait, and what's that in eternity?

Like Piccadilly Circus, if you spend long enough in our bus station cafe everyone on the world passes by, particularly everyone you know. In this case, while I wait, Carol Latham passes the window, pushing Toby. I am grateful I have a Guardian to hide behind, balanced or otherwise, as well as the steamed-up glass.

One possible life for me has come and gone: a job at the Jobcentre, leaving me with the quiet satisfaction of knowing I could have lorded it over Joker Jones, perhaps forging a ready-made family life with Carol. Another possible life just left with Glynnis on the preceding London bus. And as my own bus finally pulls into the station there is a pang, just a brief pang, of anxiety about the wisdom of turning my back on any of these options. After all, out there, out there on my own, is an unknown land full of uncertainties. And I know I am green, very green. Am I doing the right thing? No time to really question it now. The bus comes into the bay and its door swings open. The driver stands outside for tickets and luggage. I fumble for my ticket, drop my wallet and stoop to pick it up.

Then, just for a moment, I see Mum. Well what I see is my own face reflected in the chrome panel at the bottom of the bus door, slightly distorted. That makes me smile, and in that instant, I see what I have inherited besides the material things. It's the smile, her special smile.

I realise I no longer need a father. I certainly don't think I want one from the choice I am leaving behind. Of all of them, Derek the aimless drifter seems the most suitable candidate. Even if he is a myth, he is an unknown quantity I can mould into whatever character I like. Why should I bother with the real role models when I can have any dad I like? Or none? Besides, I have superior genetic gifts from Mum to make up for all that. And an echo of her voice comes to me: *Get out of this pokey little town.*

***

"Come on, hurry along now."

The bus driver is anxious to get a move on, as if he too has heard Mum's cajoling.

I mumble an apology and climb the steps. Inside I have a sudden, tightening knot of excitement.

There is hardly anyone aboard the dark upholstered interior … an elderly couple, a girl sitting alone near the back. A pretty girl with long dark hair. Just like me and Glynnis, she might be escaping a pointless little town, making herself another life. She turns for a flickering instant from looking out of the window to catch my eye, looking away again just as quickly. The doors shut and the bus lurches backwards out of the bay. It is pulling out of the station as I make my way between the seats, drawn on by an unspoken message.

I know myself. Now I do.

We are passing Woolworths, then the Prince Albert. Out of the corner of my eye another possible life comes and goes: Goldilocks is peering in WH Smiths' window, dog on a string, still cutting a romantic figure but probably doomed to roam for eternity the one-eyed community I am turning my back on. Or perhaps I am looking at a salon owner of the future... "*And what would madam like today?*"

I have a new-born confidence and the special something left to me by Mum. And with every step I take this place that has nurtured me, along with its characters and events past and recent, is shrinking, diminishing, while the big 'out there' is opening its arms wider and wider to welcome me.

I imagine I hear a soft voice: it is Beckham. I can almost see him tap the ball, watch it roll to my feet. He looks at me, raising an eyebrow.

"Your turn now, Pete. Make it a good one."

THE END

You might also enjoy these books by Ted Lamb:

Gansalaman's Gold (Kindle E-book) A dark mystery in Dracula country.

The Prophet and the Pelicans (Kindle E-book, paperback) What lies behind one of the oddest books in the Bible? Did prophet Ezekiel witness a time-tripping flight of combat helicopters many years before the birth of Christ?

Brassribs (Kindle E-book, paperback) Two generations of anglers have sought Brightwell Lake's biggest carp – but the book also tells of wartime bravery, romance and skulduggery.

Looking for Lucie (Kindle E-book, paperback) Lucie is a very, very big pike – yet while fanatical angler Mark Kendal is trying to catch her, his world is falling apart. What happens when the adversaries finally meet?

Gobblemouth (Kindle E-book, paperback) A 'problem' catfish that must be rehomed is behind this madcap road-trip across Europe to the River Danube.

The Brightwell Trilogy (Kindle E-book, paperback) The above three books – Brassribs, Looking for Lucie and Gobblemouth – are contained in this bumper edition.

Monty and the Mauler (Kindle E-book for children) Ace reporter Monty the terrier gets his canine pals together to solve a local mystery

The Fisher's Tale (Kindle E-book, paperback) Walking the pilgrim trail from France to Spain's Santiago de Compostela in 2003.

Printed in Great Britain
by Amazon